Dear Mystery Reader:

If you're looking for a new and unique mystery heroine, maybe a good laugh, or perhaps you're searching for a terrific recipe for gumbo, have I got the book for you! You're holding it in your hands right now.

Upon its hardcover publication, this series debut got all sorts excited. Mystery booksellers were recommending and hand-selling it to their customers. *People* magazine and *Entertainment Weekly* both gave it raves. And of course Nancy Bell did the people of East Texas quite proud with this tale of the outstanding and very eccentric "Biggie" Weatherford, feisty grandmother extraordinaire. The book's first printing quickly sold out.

Biggie is exactly the sort of amateur sleuth mystery readers adore: think a Texan Miss Marple with an attitude. You'll see what I mean. And when you're finished with Nancy Bell's wonderful concoction and hunger for more, fear not: Biggie's got plenty to say. There's many more books to come.

Yours in mystery,

Dana Edwin Isaacson
Senior Editor
St. Martin's DEAD LETTER Paperback Mysteries

Other titles from St. Martin's
Dead Letter Mysteries

WIN, LOSE OR DIE ed. by Cynthia Manson &
Constance Scarborough
MORTAL CAUSES by Ian Rankin
A VOW OF DEVOTION by Veronica Black
WOLF, NO WOLF by Peter Bowen
SCHOOL OF HARD KNOCKS by Donna Huston Murray
FALCONER'S JUDGEMENT by Ian Morson
WINTER GAMES by John Feinstein
THE MAN WHO INVENTED FLORIDA by Randy Wayne
White
WHISKERS AND SMOKE by Marian Babson
FLY FISHING CAN BE FATAL by David Leitz
BLACK WATER by Doug Allyn
REVENGE OF THE BARBEQUE QUEENS by Lou Jane
Temple
A MURDER ON THE APPIAN WAY by Steven Saylor
MURDER MOST BRITISH ed. by Janet Hutchings
LIE DOWN WITH DOGS by Jan Gleiter
THE CLEVELAND CONNECTION by Les Roberts
LONG SHADOWS IN VICTORY by Gregory Bean

RAVES FOR *BIGGIE AND THE POISONED POLITICIAN*

"A piquant locale...don't miss Nancy Bell's down-home East Texas debut mystery."
—Carolyn G. Hart,
author of the Death on Demand series

"Characters depicted with honesty and great flair...lovingly drawn...very successful."
—*Booklist*

"Entertaining debut...Bell's characters are painted in broad brush strokes, but their warmth and humor, equally outsized, enliven this country mystery."
—*Publishers Weekly*

"Nancy Bell's *Biggie and the Poisoned Politician* introduces us to one of the most unique narrators in modern adult mystery fiction. Nero Wolfe is back, but this time Archie Goodwin is an eleven-year-old boy named J.R. Weatherford and Nero Wolfe is a pint-sized Texas grandma named Biggie. Nancy Bell has created characters to die for."
—Susan Rogers Cooper,
author of *Doctors and Lawyers and Such*

"Biggie Weatherford is one of the most singular detectives to come along in years, but the real star is the enormously entertaining narrator, Biggie's grandson J.R. I'm eagerly anticipating a prompt return visit to Job's Crossing, Texas."
—Bill Crider, author of *Winning Can Be Murder*

"Nancy Bell's writing reminds me of Mark Twain's zestful characters...genuine charm and humor. What a delightful book!"
—Barbara Burnett Smith,
author of *Dust Devils of the Purple Sage*

Biggie
and the
Poisoned Politician

Nancy Bell

St. Martin's Paperbacks

BIGGIE AND THE POISONED POLITICIAN

Copyright © 1996 by Nancy R. Bell.

Library of Congress Catalog Card Number: 96-2636

ISBN: 0-312-96219-3

Printed in the United States of America

St. Martin's Press hardcover edition published in 1996
St. Martin's Paperbacks edition/June 1997

10 9 8 7 6 5 4 3 2 1

To Jean Houston

Acknowledgments

Many thanks to my critique group, The Shoal Creek Writers, who were so very generous in their encouragement and constructive criticism. I am especially thankful to Sharon, who believed in me long before I did. And to my agent, Roslyn Targ, who was willing to take me on even though her roster was full.

Job's Jottings from Julia

The Daughters had their regular monthly meeting at Lonie Fulkerson's house last Tuesday. The main item on the agenda was how to raise the money to repair the gazebo at the park after a certain person who shall remain nameless shot it full of holes with his shotgun. After some lovely refreshments of red punch, homemade cupcakes, and candy corn, the meeting was adjourned and we all went home. The next meeting will be at Biggie Weatherford's house sometime next month.

Speaking of Biggie Weatherford, everybody's talking about the big explosion that happened right in her driveway last week. A car belonging to Mr. Wade Hampton Crabtree, who has been living in Biggie's garage apartment for some time now, got blown to smithereens. Chief Trotter is looking into the matter. Down at the Owl Cafe they all think it might have been done by the CIA. Biggie's grandson, J.R., who was interviewed by this reporter, stated that he thought the Martians had landed.

1

The explosion ripped through the house like a west Texas tornado and caused Biggie's store-bought teeth to fall off the table and go sliding across the floor like a hockey puck. My cat, Booger, thought it was a game and started in chasing them around the room. Willie Mae ran out of the kitchen shouting, "The Day of Judgment done come! Sinners repent! Sinners repent!" Me, I crawled under the table. I thought the Martians had landed.

Biggie grabbed her teeth away from Booger, stuffed them into her mouth, and headed for the front door. Willie Mae followed Biggie, and I followed Willie Mae.

When we got to the front porch, we saw Mr. Crabtree standing by his old Buick looking like he'd just put the bucket down the well and drawn up a skunk. His coat was torn and a cut over his left eye was bleeding into his ear and dripping down on his white shirt. His Panama hat hung from a branch of Biggie's pecan tree. Papers were scattered all around his

3

car, which was nothing but a pile of black junk with little wisps of smoke rising up where the engine used to be.

Mr. Crabtree's good eye kept going back and forth from his car to Biggie, then back to his car. He opened his mouth, but no words came out, and his arms waved like a cop directing traffic. I wanted to call the doctor, but Biggie said Mr. Crabtree would be all right and made him sit on the steps and breathe into a paper sack until he could talk. When he felt better, Biggie bandaged his eye and asked what happened. You'll never guess what he said.

"The pope did it."

Willie Mae crossed herself.

"The Vatican must have heard about my work. They have spies everywhere, you know. I'll bet they had my car blown up as a warning. Oh, what shall I do, Miss Biggie? Whatever shall I do?"

Mr. Crabtree is an author and is writing a book about how the pope is planning to take over the world. He says not many people know it, but the pope already owns all the Wal-Mart stores, and that's a pretty good start right there.

To support himself until they publish his book, which will make him a millionaire and famous, Mr. Crabtree sells burial policies for the Minute Men of Freedom Insurance Company of Mobile, Alabama. That's how he met Biggie. He came to our door to sell her a peace-of-mind policy so she could sleep at night knowing her grieving loved ones would be freed from the burden of having to pay for an expensive funeral.

Biggie said she figured out the first five minutes Mr. Crabtree was there that he was a high-class gentleman on account of him being so interested when she told him about James Royce Wooten, her ancestor, who founded the town of Job's Crossing. Mr. Crabtree told Biggie right away how he used to be a member of the Sons of the Confederacy before a fast-talking Yankee from Chicago cheated him out of his daddy's money and forced him to go on the road selling burial policies.

Biggie signed up for his top-of-the-line, blue ribbon policy even though she already has a plot out at the Wooten family cemetery. She said for me to take the money and buy a nice headstone with her picture on it.

"I'm just a little boy, Biggie," I said.

"I know, honey, but you're already going on twelve, and I don't plan to go until you're big enough to handle my affairs."

When Biggie found out Mr. Crabtree had taken a room at the Big Eight Motel, she said, "Honey, you don't belong in that place. You just go get all your belongings and move into my garage apartment."

One thing I like about Mr. Crabtree is his glass eye, which he will take out and let me look at. At night he keeps it in a little miniature coffin which his company used to give away as souvenirs until the higher-ups decided it didn't project an upbeat image to be giving away coffins. Now what they give is plastic rain hats and yardsticks printed with the company name. When his ship comes in, Mr. Crabtree is going to get a new eye because the green one he has doesn't match his real eye, which is gray. When he gets his new one, he's going to give me his old eye to put on my whatnot shelf.

After Biggie got him calmed down, she told me to go in and call the police, and I did, but the line kept being busy on account of Chief Trotter being in love with Jimmie Sue Jarvis, who is deputy county clerk and the county judge's secretary and the prettiest girl in town. When Chief Trotter's not out writing parking tickets or drinking coffee at the Owl Cafe, he's talking to Jimmie Sue on the phone. Finally, Biggie said for me just to get on my bike and go over to his office and bring him right back.

The chief is a great big man with a red face who was almost drafted by the Dallas Cowboys in 1979. He would have been, too, except that Roger Staubach didn't like him on account of him being a Mormon. Roger and Tom Landry were trying to get all Baptists on the team so Billy Graham would be on their side, and how could they lose? Chief said he wouldn't compromise his beliefs for fame and fortune. Willie Mae says every time a Mormon dies, they keep their bodies in a hollowed-out mountain outside Salt Lake City. She says they've got every dead Mormon since Brigham Young in there. She says someday Donny and Marie Osmond will be there, too. I wish we were Mormons. I'd really like to see that mountain.

I was right. The chief was on the phone and didn't look too happy to be interrupted.

"What you need, J.R.?" he asked, taking his feet off the desk. "I'm right busy this afternoon."

"Biggie sent me over here to tell you to get over to our house fast," I said. "Mr. Crabtree's car got blown up and there's black stuff all over Biggie's driveway, and Mr. Crabtree's got a cut over his eye, and—"

"Speak slower, youngun," the chief said. "What do you mean, his car got blowed up? Did it overheat and catch fire?"

"No, sir. It was more like a big boom. I thought the Martians had landed, but Willie Mae thought it was the end of the world. . . ."

By that time I was talking to air, because the chief had run out of there like a sky full of greased lightning.

As I came out of the police station, which is really just a room in the jail, I spotted a stranger sitting on a bench in front of the courthouse feeding a hamburger to Ralph, the town dog. We don't get many strangers here in Job's Crossing and this one was a humdinger. He was wearing a leather jacket

6

and black boots. I saw a big, muddy Harley leaned against the statue of Biggie's ancestor, James Royce Wooten.

About that time, Jimmie Sue came out the front door of the courthouse carrying her lunch in a brown bag. She had on a real short blue skirt and a white blouse that kind of fell down off her shoulders. She sat down on the bench opposite the stranger and crossed her legs. The stranger had stopped feeding Ralph and started watching Jimmie Sue. She didn't seem to notice him there at all, just looked over at me and hollered, "Hey, J.R.! How you gettin' along?"

One thing I like about Jimmie Sue is, she has six toes on her left foot. She'd shown them to me one day at the swimming pool at the park. The sixth toe just kind of sat on top of her baby toe. She had the nail painted bright orange just like the rest of her toes.

"Ain't he cute?" she said. "I call him Winky."

I asked her if it didn't bother her when she wore shoes.

"Heck, no," she said. "See, I can just fold him under my other toes."

"Couldn't you have the doctor remove it?"

Jimmie Sue held her foot up in the air and waved it around in a circle.

"Guess I could," she said, "but then I'd be just like everybody else. This way I got something nobody else's got, see."

When I told Biggie what she'd said, Biggie said when they passed out self-esteem, Jimmie Sue was most likely the first one in line.

I grinned and waved at Jimmie Sue then hopped on my bike and rode away fast, wondering who that biker was and what he was doing in Job's Crossing. I wondered if he was a Hell's Angel and if he'd kidnap Jimmie Sue and carry her off on his big Harley and make her his woman. I saw a movie once where these bikers came into this little town and grabbed the most popular girl in high school and rode off with her. In the movie, the girl fell in love with one of the bikers and dyed her hair blond and got a tattoo that said *Buck's Woman* in a very surprising spot on her body.

When I got home, a big blue tow truck was hooked up to Mr. Crabtree's car. The chief was sitting on the porch swing drinking a glass of iced tea. Biggie was in her favorite rocking chair next to Willie Mae, who was sitting in a straight chair sewing up the hole I'd torn in my Sunday pants when I'd climbed up on the roof to get Booger down after Mrs. Moody's little white dog, Prissy, had chased him up there. I took a seat on the front steps next to Mr. Crabtree, who looked like he'd been rode hard and put up wet.

"Did anyone see or hear anything unusual before the car got blowed up? Miss Biggie, we'll start with you."

"Why, no, honey. I'd just gotten home from a meeting of the Daughters. We were discussing our fund-raiser for the year, and the meeting had become quite heated. There is a certain amount of friction among the members, don'cha know. One faction wants to elect a queen and her court from the membership and have them presented at a fancy-dress ball to be held in the VFW hall. The other faction, of which I am the leader, is pushing for a box supper and bake sale to raise the money. Our project this year is to erect a gazebo in the city park dedicated to the memory of those honorable Texans who lost their lives in the Battle of Wooten Creek. Honey, it was just exhausting. I came home and, I believe, may have dropped off to sleep in my chair."

"You did, Biggie. You were snoring away," I said.

Then the chief said, "What about you, Willie Mae?"

"No, sir. I didn't exactly what you'd call *hear* anything. I was peeling peaches for a cobbler for tonight's supper. What it was was I actually *felt* something. The whole house shook when that there car went up. I thought the communists had come and dropped a A-bomb on us. That's what I thought."

"No, you did not, Willie Mae," I said. "You thought it was the end of the world. I heard you."

"Well, Mr. Smarty. Who thought the Martians had landed? Huh?"

The chief wiped his face with a big red hanky.

"Miss Biggie, I wonder if I might have just a little more of this here excellent iced tea. Four spoons of sugar, if you don't mind. Now, Mr. Crabtree, since it was your vehicle, what are your thoughts on this matter?"

"I think it's a sad state of affairs when a man can't leave his own car parked in his own driveway without having it bombed off the face of the earth. Whatever am I to do? My car's my livelihood!"

"Do you know anyone who might have it in for you?"

"Only the pope."

While the chief was thinking that over, Booger came running across the porch chasing a pecan. I thought Mr. Crabtree was going to jump right out of his skin.

"Shades of Stonewall Jackson," he said. "I'm just a bundle of raw nerves."

Biggie came out of the house and handed the chief his tea. She patted Mr. Crabtree on the shoulder. "Never mind, honey," she said. "We'll find out who did this and make them pay. You just answer all Chief Trotter's questions."

The chief pulled a little spiral notebook out of his pocket and started making notes.

"Now, then, Mr. Crabtree, I know your current address is back there in Miss Biggie's garage apartment. Would you please state your full name and where you came from?"

"My name is Wade Hampton Crabtree of Tupelo, Mississippi."

"And would you please state your age?"

"I'm fifty-eight—born on the twelfth of February. In my younger days, I took a lot of ribbing due to being born on the birthday of the Great Emancipator. Back then, Mr. Lincoln was still viewed by many in the South with some animosity. I got 'em back, though. All I had to do was remind 'em whose name I proudly bear, that of a fine Confederate general. General Wade Hampton of the Charleston Hamptons!"

"Are you married?"

"No, sir. I have never known the joys of matrimony. Always been something of a vagabond. It's hard to hit a moving target, is what I always say."

"Mr. Crabtree, do you have any family? Brothers or sisters, I mean?"

"Now, honey," Biggie said, "do you have to know all this? I'm sure Mr. Crabtree's tired and upset. Can't you get to the point?"

"Beg your pardon, Miss Biggie, but I know my business. Just routine questions, don'cha know."

Mr. Crabtree sighed. "Continue, Chief."

"Brothers or sisters?"

"Alas, no. My dear mother almost died giving birth to me and suffered from a prolapsed womb and deep depression for the remainder of her life. My father, being a true gentleman of the old school, restrained his passions after my birth."

"And how far did you go in school? High school? College?"

"Four years prep school and six at Washington and Lee," Mr. Crabtree said. "Although, unfortunately, my father yanked me from school before I was granted a degree."

"You went to college for six years and never graduated?"

"Exactly what my father said. Mother and I both thought

he was unfeeling to halt my studies so abruptly. I was forced to join him in his business endeavors."

"And what might those be?"

Mr. Crabtree waved his hand.

"Quite diverse, actually. Cotton mostly, but he had holdings in mining and tobacco, as well as a large shrimping operation in the Gulf."

The chief stood up. "That oughta do it for now. We'll put all our efforts into solving this crime, Mr. Crabtree. Don't you worry about a thing."

Mr. Crabtree went out in the yard and started gathering up his papers that had flown all over the place, mumbling to himself about his life's work going up in one fell swoop. He stuffed them in his pockets and started around back toward his garage apartment.

"You get some rest, honey," Biggie called after him. "There's nothing so bad it can't be fixed."

After he was gone, Biggie turned to the chief. "What are your ideas on this, honey?" she asked.

"It's a mystery, Miss Biggie. A pure-dee mystery. We ain't had a vehicle bombed here since Elmore Guthrie was blastin' stumps and blew his tractor to smithereens. I'll work on it, though. You'll let me know if you hear anything, won't you?"

"You bet, Chief. I'll be working on it, too."

After supper, which was chicken and dumplings, my favorite, I asked Biggie why she thought Chief Trotter was asking Mr. Crabtree all those questions.

"He seemed like he thought he blew up his own car," I said.

"No, honey, that's not it at all. If I know Travis Trotter, he was just finding out all he could about poor Mr. Crabtree so he could go down to the Owl Cafe tomorrow and tell all his cronies about the stranger Biggie Weatherford's got living in her garage apartment. The whole town's been curious as a tree full of monkeys ever since he came here."

Just then, Willie Mae came into the room. "Miss Biggie, I'm going over to Rosebud's and take him some of this leftover peach cobbler. You need anything while I'm out?"

"No, thanks, honey," Biggie said. "You just run along—and tell Rosebud the azaleas need pruning."

2

Willie Mae's not the first maid Biggie's ever had, but she's the first that would ever stay. Biggie says they're sisters under the skin. I say it *must* be *un*der the skin, because Willie Mae's the blackest woman I've ever seen and Biggie's the whitest. Her hair's white, her skin's white, and she has these real light blue eyes that can look in your head and tell exactly what you're thinking. Willie Mae's a voodoo woman. If Biggie's not reading my mind, Willie Mae will scare me to death by telling me she'll do voodoo on me if I don't act right. You can see I don't get away with much around our house.

Biggie says we're real lucky to have Willie Mae on account of good help is hard to find. The way Biggie used to find someone to clean up the house and cook for us was to drive her car down to Harlem Heights and stop women on the street and ask them if they wanted a job. If they said yes, she'd just open the car door and they'd get in and come home with us and do housework for a few hours.

The first maid we had was named Codella. I'll never forget the day she came to work for us. We'd been fishing at Wooten Creek. I caught a turtle but Biggie wouldn't let me take him home on account of him being an alligator snapper. She said they can tear your finger off in one bite and swallow it down before a cat can lick his fanny. Biggie was lucky. She caught a catfish that must of weighed upwards of five pounds. Biggie pulled him out and looked at him.

"Well, I'll be switched," she said, "that fish looks mighty like Osbert Gribbons."

I had to agree with her. Mr. Gribbons is our mayor, and he *does* have a big mouth and little bitty eyes set wide apart on his head. When Biggie took him off the hook, that old fish stuck his fin in her hand.

"Guess he didn't like that remark," she said. "Hand me that bottle of rubbing alcohol out of the tackle box, J.R. I knew a man once who got finned by a catfish. His hand turned black as a well digger's pocket and he lost three fingers and part of his thumb."

Biggie poured the alcohol on her hand and made a face. "Ouch, that smarts," she said.

"Biggie," I said, "that old fish looks like he's laughing at you."

"Maybe he is, son. Maybe he is."

When we got home, Biggie said for me to put that fish in the toilet in the hall bathroom because we had to go find us a maid on account of she had to get to her bridge club on time.

We got in Biggie's car and drove over to Harlem Heights.

Pretty soon we saw Codella walking down the road singing "Joshua Fit the Battle of Jericho." Biggie pulled up beside her and rolled down the window.

"Honey," she called, "do you want to come over to my house and help me this afternoon?"

Codella came over to the car and leaned down so she could

14

look in the window. She was very tall and had on a straw sun hat with a bumper sticker for a hatband. It said HONK IF YOU LOVE JESUS.

"How much you pay?" she said.

"Honey, I'll pay you five dollars an hour—and I've got some really nice clothes for you, too. Hardly look like they've been worn."

Codella looked at Biggie, who is five feet tall and not much bigger than a minute.

"Don't reckon I could get into your clothes. What else you got?"

"Well . . ." said Biggie. "Oh, I know! I've got a really fine piece of jewelry I can give you. It's a genuine imitation diamond brooch that I got for Christmas last year from J.R.'s mama. I don't know why she gave it to me. She knows I don't wear jewelry. It's still in the box. How about that?"

Biggie and Codella talked a while longer and, after Biggie promised the earrings that matched the brooch, Codella got in the car.

When we got back home, Biggie said, "Now, honey, I've got to get to my bridge club. You just clean up the house real good and do up that little bitty stack of ironing over there on the table."

"Didn't nobody say nothin' about no ironing," Codella said. "I charge extra for that."

Biggie offered to give her some cuttings from her rose-bushes. "I won a blue ribbon at the State Fair of Texas for my Shirley Temple," she said. "You can't find roses like that just anywhere."

"Huh," Codella said.

"Well, then how about a nice winter coat?" Biggie said. "It belonged to my former husband, Cuthbert P. Weatherford, who only wore the finest hand-tailored clothing."

"Miss Biggie," Codella said, "everybody in town knows

your husband ain't been seen around here since the Korean War. That there coat prob'ly be eat up by moths by now. All I gotta say is, if you wants that there ironing done, you gonna have to come up with some cash money."

Biggie finally agreed to pay what Codella asked for and hurried out the door saying the girls were going to be awfully mad on account of her being late for bridge.

After Biggie left, I went into the living room to watch television. I could hear Codella out in the kitchen singing. After a while, I got tired of watching and went in to talk to Codella.

"Codella," I said, "how do you 'fit' a battle? Do they come in sizes?"

Codella looked at me like I had a tail and went to clean the bathroom. I went out on the front porch and sat on the swing. Pretty soon I heard Codella screaming her head off.

"The devil himself! Lordy mercy! Lordy mercy! Old devil be in this house!"

She ran out the front door and into the front yard. Booger happened to be on the sidewalk watching a squirrel up in the pecan tree. I guess Codella didn't see him because she tripped over him and fell down. Booger jumped on the porch rail and started in licking himself real hard. Codella picked herself up and ran off down the street yelling, "I seen him! I seen the devil!"

When Biggie got back, I told her what had happened.

"Poor thing, she must be crazy," she said. "Never mind. Run in the bathroom and get me that catfish so I can clean him for supper."

When I went to get the fish, I found a big mess in the bathroom. The mop bucket had overturned and water was all over the floor and spilling out on Biggie's carpet in the hall. The cleanser and glass cleaner had spilled and mixed in with the mop water. That old fish had managed to get himself scrunched down the hole in the toilet so only his head was showing. I guess he was plenty mad about it, because he was glaring up at me out of the water.

He tasted mighty good, though. While we were eating, I asked Biggie, "Reckon why Codella ran off like that, Biggie?"

"I don't know, son," she said. "We'll go on over there tomorrow and see if we can find someone not so high-strung to help us."

The next day, Biggie brought home Shanelle. I liked her; she was young. She wore her hair in those little bitty braids all over her head and would let me feel of it.

One day she said, "J.R., do you know how to dance?"

"Uh-uh," I said.

"Want me to teach you?"

"I guess so," I said.

She turned on the TV to the rock channel.

"Now, watch what I do."

That Shanelle was all over the place. Boy, could she dance. Pretty soon I was dancing just as good as anybody. Shanelle said, for a white boy, I was pretty good.

One morning, she came to work looking like she'd have to get better to die.

"Miss Biggie," she said about two o'clock, "I believe I'm gonna have to go in the spare room and rest a minute. I feel real bad."

Biggie said that was okay but take her crocheted bedspread off the bed on account of her grandmother had made that when she was only fourteen years old and it was a valuable family heirloom. It sure is a good thing she did, because it wasn't long before we heard a funny sound coming out of the spare room. Biggie sent me in to see about it. I wish she hadn't of done that. I'm too young to see such things. Blood was all over the place, and Shanelle was sitting up in the bed looking real surprised. She was holding a little bitty baby.

"Miss Biggie," she said later, "I swear on a thousand Bibles, I didn't know I was carrying a baby."

Biggie said she felt real bad about it, but a person that didn't know if she was pregnant or not couldn't be too reliable, so she had to let Shanelle go.

The next woman, I don't remember her name, but it doesn't matter because she didn't even stay long enough to take her hat off. When she saw Biggie sitting in the kitchen with her feet in the refrigerator, she just walked straight on through the house and out the back door. As she left, I heard her say something about how everybody said that there Biggie Weatherford was crazy, and they was right. Biggie says, why spend good money on air-conditioning when the fridge works just as good and don't take near as much electricity.

Mama says Biggie's crazy to let just anyone in her house that she doesn't even know. She says one day we'll wake up murdered in our beds and all Biggie's mama's silver will be gone. I say if we're murdered in our beds silver will be the least of our worries. Biggie says she's a good judge of character and never lets anyone help in the house if she doesn't have a good feeling about them.

Willie Mae came on her own. We didn't have to go to Harlem Heights to find her. She just showed up at our door one day with all her stuff in a tow sack.

"Here I am," was all she said.

Biggie invited her in and the two of them sat down at the kitchen table and drank coffee and talked for the longest time. Biggie says she and Willie Mae are soul sisters and it was karma that brought Willie Mae to us.

Willie Mae told Biggie all about how she learned to be a voodoo woman from Sister Arthusia Sylvester down in the bayou country. She said folks don't mess with her much because she knows African voodoo, which is the strongest there

18

is. She told me she once put a really serious voodoo curse on a woman who stole her man by leaving a white handkerchief on her front porch. If you find a white handkerchief on your porch, watch out, somebody in the house is going to die. Sure enough, that woman's oldest son got drunk and fell in a cistern that very night. They found him the next morning, not dead, but so scared he couldn't talk for three days. Willie Mae said she left them alone after that, but it was a warning. If that woman had ever messed with her man again, she would of got her good.

"Whatever happened to your man, Willie Mae?" I asked.

"The law's taken him. He's in the jailhouse in Morgan City, Louisiana."

"If I was a voodoo woman, I'd make up a spell to get him out," I said.

"If a bullfrog had wings, he wouldn't bump his ass every time he hopped," she said. "Now, get on out of here and let me do my work."

Biggie says Willie Mae's voodoo is a God-given talent. She says someday she and Willie Mae are going to have a séance to raise the spirit of old James Royce. He can tell her all the things that happened back in history that didn't get written down. Then she can present a paper to the Daughters that will make her a legend in her own time. In the meantime, she says Willie Mae is the best help she's ever had.

Biggie cleaned out the guest house, which is a little bitty house out in the backyard, and Willie Mae moved right in. The first thing she did was pull a picture of the Virgin Mary out of her sack and hang it on the wall. Then she lined up all her potions and spell powders on a shelf right under it. She covered the bed with a silk shawl with long gold fringe and decorated with a green dragon.

"Where'd you get that, Willie Mae?" I asked. "It's pretty."

"It was given to me by Sister Sylvester when I finished my

training," she said. "It's my most prized possession. It has the Power."

"What power?"

"Never mind. One of these days, maybe you'll see."

Now that Willie Mae is here, our house is always clean and the pile of dirty clothes by the washer has disappeared. Another thing I like is her cooking. Biggie can fry up a mess of catfish and she makes real good squirrel stew, but just don't ever let her fry you an egg. The yolks are so hard you can't even get your fork in them. Biggie says she learned all the cooking she knows on camping trips with her daddy and his friends. She says she never was much for cooking and keeping a house nice and that's why having Willie Mae here is God's gift from heaven. Willie Mae's fried chicken is so crispy your mouth doesn't know when to stop, and her sweet potato pie will make you slap your grandpa. Now I go around as full as a tick on a boar hog. Last week, Willie Mae had to let all my pants out.

Willie Mae had been at our house about a month when her husband, Rosebud Robichaux, knocked on our back door. He said they'd let him out of jail early on account of he was the best prisoner they'd ever had in the Morgan City jailhouse. He said the sheriff said he couldn't figure out why they ever incarcerated such an upstanding man as him in the first place.

I was just finishing lunch when he came into our kitchen. His clothes were all dirty and torn and, to tell the truth, he smelled more like a wet dog in a bait shop than a rosebud. He laughed when he saw me put my hand over my nose and said the reason he smelled so bad was because when he was a little boy, his mama made him eat rutabagas every single day of his life. It messed up his system, he said, so now he always smells like turnips even right after he gets out of the bathtub. Willie Mae didn't say anything, just made him go out to her little house and take off all his clothes. He had to sit there wrapped up in a blanket while she washed them.

Rosebud has these real cool gold hearts and clubs and diamonds and spades built right into his four front teeth. He won them playing poker with a dentist. Rosebud said it was either that, or he took the dentist's chair to pay off the bet. Willie Mae says, when she married Rosebud he was making good money shooting craps on Bourbon Street, but then he got to messing with women and went bad on her. She wouldn't let him move into her little house with her until he'd proved he'd changed his ways, so he had to rent a room down at Mrs. Ola Mae Gandy's Ritzy Lodge Boarding House.

Biggie liked Rosebud right away and decided he would be perfect to take care of the yard and keep her car in good shape.

"Honey," she said, "do you think you could tend to my flower beds?"

"Well, Miss Biggie, you might say, in a manner of speaking, I happen to be known all over the State of Louisiana as a mighty good gardener."

"Can you prune my roses?"

"In answer to that, Miss Biggie, I am not one to be known as what you might call a braggable person, but I once won a blue ribbon from the mayor of Lake Charles. I believe they said it was for my rose pruning. I'd have to say that I'm known all over the bayou country for my rose pruning."

Biggie hired him on the spot. She said a man that full of hot air must be good for something. As it turned out, it was the smartest thing she ever did.

Biggie was right about Chief Trotter telling everybody in town about our big explosion. The phone kept ringing off the wall with people wanting to find out all about Mr. Crabtree's car. Finally Biggie had enough. "Come on," she said, "it looks like we're going to have to go fishing to get away from the telephone."

We all got in Biggie's car and drove out to Wooten Creek. I got twenty-seven tadpoles in a jar which I'm going to start a frog farm with. Rosebud says there's good money in frog legs. I'm going to take the money and buy Biggie a big red car so everybody in town will see her coming and get out of the way on account of she's going to hit somebody someday the way she drives. She's already knocked over just about every mailbox in the county.

That night, Biggie said tomorrow we'd drive out to the farm on account of she had a real hankering for some fresh tomatoes and turnip greens.

3

Biggie still owns the farm she grew up on, but now Mr. Sontag and his wife and his daughter, Monica, live there. Monica has no hair on one side of her head on account of being left too close to the fire when she was a baby. I like going to the farm. Me and Monica play War of the Space Giants in the hayloft. Monica is good as Fracton King of the Martians because of her half-bald head. I play Commander Corey of the Spaceship *Nebula*.

Mr. Sontag is tall, thin as a mashed snake, and has one front tooth missing. I like to see him spit tobacco juice through his gap. He can hit a dragonfly at ten yards. Mrs. Sontag is really fat. Mr. Sontag says she's warm in winter and shade in summer, which I think shows he has a real good attitude. Some men might not like to have a wife as fat as Mrs. Sontag. She has the reddest hair I ever saw. Biggie says she dyes it with henna, which is a plant and looks like cow manure when you put it on but turns hair red.

"Hidy, Coye," Biggie shouted from the car. "Got any greens today?"

Mr. Sontag nodded his head and grinned. He knows there's nothing in the world Biggie loves more than turnip greens unless it's turnip greens and chitlins, which, if you knew what that was, it would turn your stomach.

"You want turnip or mustard?" Mr. Sontag asked. "Collards ain't made yet."

"Think I'll have a little of both," Biggie said, "and some of those nice cherry tomatoes if you've got um."

Mr. Sontag spat a stream of tobacco juice at a grasshopper sitting on the fence post. "I'll go get a bucket," he said.

"Wait just a minute, Coye," Biggie said. "As we turned onto your road, I saw some 'dozers working over on the Plummer place. Know what they're doing over there?"

Mr. Sontag spit out his chew, then pulled out a bag of Red Man tobacco and stuffed another big wad into his mouth. "Well'm, 'pears to me like somebody said they was buildin' whatcha call one of them sanitarium landfills."

"What?"

"A sanitarium landfill, don'cha know? Where they dump the trash."

"Coye, are you telling me they're building a *dump* right next door to this farm?"

"Yes'm, I reckon so," Mr. Sontag said. "I seen the mayor and that there Mr. Thripp over there day before yestiddy. They come over here and ask my wife for a drink of water and I asked um, I said, whatchall doin' over yonder, and they said we's buildin' a dump for the city. I told um, I said, Miss Biggie ain't gonna like that."

Biggie shook her head so hard I thought her glasses were going to fall right off her face.

"We'll just see about that. Yessiree. We'll see about that. Why, that's right next to the Wooten family graveyard."

24

"Biggie," I said, "can me and Monica go play in the woods?"

"Sure, honey," she said without even looking at me. "I'll just sit here on the porch and visit with Coye and Ernestine for a while. We've got some mighty important things to discuss. Y'all kids go on and play."

"What you wanta do?" Monica asked as we headed down the cow path toward the woods.

"Wanta make a grapevine swing?" I asked.

"Guess we could—or we could go down to the creek and catch crawdads."

"Or go skinny-dippin'," I said.

"Or all three!"

It ended up we didn't do any of those things. Monica's old dog, Buster, was runnin' circles from us to the woods and back. All of a sudden we heard Buster barking to beat the band.

"Reckon what's the matter with that there dog?" Monica said. "He don't generally bark like that."

"Must of got a possum treed," I said. "Let's go look!"

We took off through the woods toward the sound of Buster's barks, but it seemed like he kept getting farther and farther away. Pretty soon, Monica flopped down under a tree.

"I gotta rest," she said.

I sure was glad she said that, because my tongue was hangin' out like a huntin' dog. We lay back on some moss and didn't talk for a while. Buster's voice kept gettin' fainter and fainter. Then it stopped.

Monica raised up on one elbow.

"You hear anything?" she asked.

"Naw."

"Reckon what's happened?"

"Maybe he's diggin' after a skunk. If he is, we better get outta here."

"No. Buster's too smart for that. He got sprayed one time. Momma pretty near washed all his hide off with lye soap. He ain't been after a skunk since."

"Listen," I said. "You hear that?"

Real faint, off in the distance, I heard old Buster bayin' like a bloodhound.

"He ever holler like that?"

Monica jumped up.

"No. He's in trouble. Come on!"

We ran through the woods for what seemed like a mile or more, but it couldn't have been on account of those woods aren't that big. I was getting scratched all over with briars and once Monica fell down and cut her knee on a root.

"Buster!" Monica called. "Buster. Momma's comin', honey."

She was way ahead of me when, all of a sudden, she stopped dead.

"Oh my gracious," she said. "Oh my gosh!" She was panting like a lizard on a hot rock and looking down.

"Look!" she said, pointing down.

I looked, and there was the biggest and deepest hole I'd ever seen right at our feet. I could barely see Buster down in the bottom, going crazy, jumping and crying.

"What are we gonna do, J.R.," she said. "How we gonna get Buster out?"

It was plain as day that I was going to have to think of something, being the man and all. And for the life of me I couldn't think of a way in the world to get that dog out of that hole.

"If we had a rope . . ."

Monica was jumping up and down by now.

"We ain't got a rope, J.R. What we gonna do? Look at 'im. He's panic struck!"

"Well, I'm gettin' a little panic struck myself. How 'bout if we get one of those grapevines and run it down to him?"

"What's he gonna do, shinny up it with his hands? Dogs can't climb a vine, J.R."

I walked around the hole a little bit and tried to figure out how we were going to get old Buster out of there. The hole was a good ten feet across and must of been that deep with straight sides covered with red clay. It was a cinch old Buster would never be able to get himself out of there. I was scratching my head and wondering who'd want to dig a hole like that when I got an idea.

"Monica," I said, "look over there. There's a road leadin' past this hole. Must be a old loggin' road. And, over there's a brush pile. Treetops, most likely. Now, here's what me and you can do. We can throw those treetops down in the hole until there's a big enough pile down there and then we can keep on calling old Buster until maybe he'll get the idea to climb up um and get out that way."

"Let's get to work," Monica said. "It's breakin' my heart to hear my baby cryin' like that."

It took us the better part of an hour to get that hole filled up with treetops. Old Buster seemed to know what we were doing because every time a new branch would fall in, he'd climb right up on top of the pile. When the stack finally got tall enough for him to scramble out, he was so happy he peed all over our feet. When we got back to the house, Biggie was still sitting on the porch drinking coffee and talking to Mrs. Sontag.

Buster jumped up on Mrs. Sontag's lap and started licking her all over—like he was trying to tell her about his big adventure.

"Get off me, dog," she hollered. "Now looky here, you've gone and got black stuff all over my apron!"

"We gotta go," Biggie said, and stood up.

When we got to the car, Mrs. Sontag said, "Biggie, did Coye tell you about them men comin' out here wantin' to lease this farm?"

"What did you say, Ernestine?"

"They was a man come out here, let's see, musta been six or eight weeks ago. Said he was from some big minin' company. Wanted to lease this place for lignite, whatever that is."

"Well, I think lignite might be some kind of coal, but I never heard of anybody mining that here in Kemp County. What did the man look like?"

"Kinda smallish. Fancy dresser. Had on a black cowboy hat and boots and one of them belts with a big silver buckle on it. Said he was leasin' up all the land in this here part of the county and we was all gonna be rich. Coye told him he guessed as how we wasn't gonna be rich on account of we didn't own this place. Told him he'd have to talk to you but it wouldn't do him no good 'cause you didn't lease to nobody."

"You're mighty right about that," Biggie said. "Mighty right! As long as I'm alive and kicking, nobody's going to come on this property punching holes and scraping up the ground. If he comes back, you let me know. You hear? Right now, I've got to get to work to get that dump dismantled. I'm not going to spend eternity right next to a trash heap!"

Biggie hurried up and got her vegetables in the car. I didn't hardly get a chance to say good-bye to Monica. On the way out the driveway, Biggie knocked over the Sontags' mailbox. She rolled down the window and hollered she'd pay for it.

As soon as we got home, Biggie went to work.

"Willie Mae," she said, "put these greens in the bathtub to soak and come on in here. We've got work to do."

They sat down at the dining table and started right in planning. Biggie wanted Willie Mae to cook up one of her voodoo spells to get rid of the dump.

"Miss Biggie," Willie Mae said, "I haven't never put no spells on no *land* before. I mostly just do it to folks—not anything that ain't what you'd call alive. I did put a hex on a cow once. She wouldn't let her milk down. What I did was—"

"Never mind about that right now," Biggie said. "We've got to think of something."

"Well, I guess we could try the rattlesnake-venom-and-sarsperilla cure. I did that on a undertaker oncet. Feller fell in a open grave and passed from the heebie-jeebies before they found him. You reckon that grave could pass for land?"

"You're the witch doctor, Willie Mae. What else you got?"

"They was the time my mama's uncle's third wife stole a pistol from me. I got her with ground-up red ants in her gumbo."

Biggie sighed.

"Willie Mae, we're talking about a garbage dump here, not some petty theft. You keep working on it until you come up with something. What's that black stuff all over the rug? Didn't you vacuum this morning?"

Willie Mae looked down at the floor. "My sakes," she said. "That wasn't here this morning. Lemme see your feet, boy."

Sure enough, black stuff was all over the bottoms of my shoes.

"Where you get that?" Willie Mae said. "Take them shoes off. Leave them on the porch 'til I can clean them."

"It must of come from the hole," I said. Then I told them about Buster getting trapped and us having to rescue him.

"Let me see that shoe," Biggie said. "We don't have black dirt here in Kemp County. This is red clay country." She rubbed her finger on the sole of my shoe and held it up. "I wonder," she said, "I just wonder. . . ."

"What, Biggie?" I said.

"I wonder if that might be some of that coal Ernestine was talking about. Oh, well, never mind. It's probably not important. Right now, I'm just interested in getting rid of that dump the city's gone and put next to my farm. Tomorrow we'll go down to city hall and tell Mayor Osbert Gribbons where the cow ate the cabbage."

"Can I go, Biggie?" I asked.

"Sure," Biggie said. "You're my partner, aren't you?"

4

Biggie is called Biggie because when I was little I couldn't say "Big Mama." I guess I must of started something because now everybody in town calls her Biggie. She says she doesn't mind except when Dwight Spofford, who sacks groceries at the Piggly Wiggly, calls her that because Dwight is just a kid and should show some respect. She says he ought to call her Miss Biggie.

"I'm just a kid, too, Biggie," I said.

"That's different. You're family."

Biggie's big on family. She's president of the Daughters because of her ancestor, James Royce Wooten, who I'm named after. He came to Texas with Stephen F. Austin and was our very first settler . . . white, that is. There were a lot of Indians already here but Biggie says, to the Daughters they don't count. The reason James Royce stopped in east Texas instead of going all the way to Austin with the rest of the colony was boils. He had a bad case. They wouldn't go away even when he put raw bacon on them to draw the pus out. The minute one boil would heal, two more would pop up somewhere else on his body. Somewhere in Arkansas he got one on his behind. That did it. Soon after they crossed the Red River into Texas, he unloaded his wagon and set up camp.

"I'm wore to a frazzle and sick as a poisoned pup and I ain't ridin' one more mile," he said.

That night he took a bath in the creek, and the next morning his boils were all gone. He built a cabin in a big piney grove right beside the creek, and from that day on old James Royce never had another boil. He started a town and called it Job's Crossing on account of this being where his boils were healed. Pretty soon he married Eleanor Ann Muckleroy, who was the prettiest girl in town, which wasn't saying much on account of there were only three. One was already married and the other was sixty-seven years old. James Royce never left Kemp County after that except for the time he had to go down to San Jacinto and help General Houston beat the tar out of Santa Ana. After the war, he and Eleanor Ann built a big house on the hill where the family graveyard now sits, and had themselves eight kids.

Two years ago, I came to live with Biggie in Job's Crossing. I used to live with Mama and Daddy in Dallas until Mama divorced Daddy for going to happy hour every single day after work and leaving her with nobody to talk to but me. After the divorce, Mama sent me to live with Biggie and she took a job at Southwestern Title. Now she gets to go to happy hour. She sent me a jigger glass with a picture of the Dallas skyline. I let my hamster, Hopalong, drink out of it.

Biggie says Daddy never should have married Mama in the first place because it would take a special kind of person to appreciate his natural joy-dee-veever and high-spirited nature and, heaven knew, Mama was not that person. Biggie says when Daddy was a young man, every girl for four counties wanted to marry him. She said she never did see what it was he saw in Mama, who was a Yankee from Kansas that he'd met while he was in the army. Biggie says everybody knows Yankees don't have a sense of humor.

Before Daddy died last year, he used to say as soon as he could get on his feet he was going to let me come live with him. Mama said over her dead body. Anyway, she said he'd never get on his feet because he spent everything he made on bar flies, which I don't believe for one minute, because who would spend money on flies? Mama says demon rum got him in the end.

Daddy used to lease portable toilets to construction sites. Mama said she was so embarrassed she couldn't hold her head up in front of the neighbors when Daddy would park his truck in front of our house all loaded up with plastic toilets. Daddy said if it wasn't for toilets, she wouldn't have a house.

I think what *really* made her divorce him was because of the time Daddy and his friend, Otis Pharr, had been drinking beer all day and decided to play a joke on Mama. They went over to Otis's sign shop and made up a magnetic sign and stuck it on the side of Daddy's truck. It said: IT MAY BE YOUR SHIT—BUT IT'S MY BREAD AND BUTTER. When Mama saw it, she took a sick headache and had to go to bed for a week.

Biggie never has sick headaches or any other kind of headaches. She says the reason she's so healthy is on account of being born and bred in the country. She grew up on a farm, the very same farm where James Royce got his boils healed.

Her daddy taught her to plow as soon as she could walk, and by the time she was five she could already drive a team of mules. She could make those mules dance a two-step just by talking to them. She says it's a God-given talent, being

33

good with animals. She could make a cow give milk just by setting the bucket under her and waiting for the milk to come squirting out. Once she was demonstrating her no-hands milking at the county fair when a train came by. The cow got so excited she started jumping around and before long she was squirting butter all over the place.

Once Biggie taught her mother's chickens to lay square eggs so her mama could just line them up in pasteboard boxes to take to town to sell.

Mama says I shouldn't believe half what Biggie says because she's just as full of bull as her son was. She says if her own mother would of had enough sense to stay in Kansas instead of running off to Montana with a rodeo clown, I could of stayed with her. She says she hopes living with a crazy old woman like Biggie won't cause me to grow up to be a drinker and a woman chaser like my daddy.

Mama doesn't know it, but I'm going to be an astronaut like Commander Corey of the Star Forces of the Universe. I don't think he even knows any women except Terry Peterson, his loyal assistant—and he doesn't drink anything but Big Cee fruit punch. He drinks that all the time to keep his strength up for space missions.

This afternoon, I pretended I was clearing the area where two spaceships collided. What I was really doing was cleaning up the mess in the yard where Mr. Crabtree's car exploded. He'd already gathered up all his papers and the stuff he wanted to keep, so all I had to do was rake up the burnt leaves and grass and then hose off the driveway. Biggie was sitting on the front porch watching to see that I did a good job, like she always does. While I was raking around the gardenia bush, I found something shiny.

"What's this, Biggie?" I asked, holding it up so she could see.

"Bring it over here, J.R. I can't see it," Biggie said.

It was a silver, ruffledy thing with two holes in the middle. Biggie held it out from her eyes as far as her arm could reach because her eyes are not as good as they used to be.

"It's a silver Mexican concho," she said. "They're used for decorating things like belts and saddles and such. I believe I'll just hold on to this. It might be a clue." She took the concho in and put it in her jewelry box.

The next day me and Biggie went downtown to talk to Chief Trotter about the crime. Biggie decided we'd drive to town even though our house is only two blocks from the square.

"It looks like it's about to cloud up and rain," she said. "We might just as well take the car."

When Biggie drives her car to town, everybody knows to get out of the way because Biggie doesn't believe in stepping on the brake pedal until she gets where she's going. Mama says she's a menace behind the wheel of a car and she just hopes Biggie doesn't kill somebody before the law gets smart enough to take her license away. Truth is, Biggie hasn't had a driver's license since 1954, when she had her purse snatched right in front of Neiman Marcus's store in downtown Dallas when she was just going in to buy a new hat for Easter.

When we got to the chief's office, Norman Thripp, the city manager, was sitting in a chair next to the chief. They were looking at some papers on the desk. When he saw Biggie, Mr. Thripp's face got all puckered up like he'd just taken a big bite out of a green persimmon.

" 'Morning, Miss Biggie—J.R.," he said. "We're a little busy right now. Discussing the police budget, don'cha know. Wonder if you folks could come back a little later?"

"Don't mind if I do," said Biggie, taking a chair and pulling it up to the desk where they were sitting. "J.R., you just sit over on that couch and read a magazine."

"Er, Miss Biggie, perhaps you didn't hear—"

"I heard you, Norman," Biggie said, "but seeing as how the police budget doesn't to much more than the light bill, gas for the police car, and coffee money for the chief, I didn't think you'd mind if I just sat here and waited. It couldn't take much longer than you could hold a bear by the tail."

"Well—well, then, perhaps we'll just finish this later." Mr. Thripp gathered up his papers and stood up.

He's very tall and has a little knobby head and ears that look like a taxicab with the doors open. His hair's almost gone, but what he has left he lets grow real long and coils it around his head. His eyes look like silver ball bearings—you know, hard and cold.

I could tell he was mad, but Biggie didn't seem to notice.

"How's Mattie?" she asked. "You two still engaged to be engaged?"

"Miss Mattie's fine—fine," he said, edging toward the door. "Yes, Miss Biggie. We're still seeing each other. Nothing serious, y'understand. Just the best of pals."

"Yes, well, I'm not sure Mattie feels that way about it. Just don't you break her heart, Norman Thripp, or I'll be on you like ugly on an ape."

"Why, Miss Biggie. I—"

"Good-bye, now," Biggie said, "and tell Osbert Gribbons I'll be coming to see him about that eyesore you people have dug out by the Wooten family graveyard." Biggie waved her hand and turned to the chief as the door slammed behind Mr. Thripp.

"Now, Chief, what have you got on our crime?"

"Not a whole lot, Miss Biggie. There's a stranger in town—

a motorcycle type. Been hanging around the courthouse a lot. I think he's sweet on Jimmie Sue, myself."

"Have you questioned him?"

"Yes, ma'am. Brought him in this morning. Couldn't keep him, though. Only connection between him and Crabtree is, they both come from southern states—not even the same state. Biker guy's from Tennessee."

"I saw him, Biggie," I said. "He was feeding Ralph."

"Anything else?" Biggie asked, ignoring me.

"No, ma'am. That's about all, except that I ran a check on Crabtree, and he seems like he's telling the truth. Used to be well off until 'long about nineteen eighty-two, when he had to declare bankruptcy. He was only able to keep one of his companies, but it wasn't doing good."

"What company was that?"

"It was called Crabtree Energy Company of West Virginia—"

Just then I remembered something.

"Biggie!" I said. "Guess what? You know that concho I found in the yard?"

Biggie pulled it out of her purse and laid it on the desk.

"What about it?"

"I saw one just like that. It was on the saddlebags on that biker's motorcycle. They were black with leather fringe and they had silver conchos on the flap. I remember, Biggie!"

"Well, well," said the chief. "I guess I'll just have to have another talk with him. Where'd you find this?"

"Right in our driveway," I said. "Didn't I, Biggie?"

"You sure did, honey," she said. "Now, let's you and me go on home and let the chief get about his business. You will let me know what you find, won't you, Chief?"

"You bet, Miss Biggie. I can always use your help. You know that."

After we left the police station, Biggie and I walked down the sidewalk past Butch's Flower Salon and Itha's House of Hair to Mattie's Tea Room. I hate it. I don't think Commander Corey would be caught dead in a place like that. Biggie drags me in there all the time because Miss Mattie's a friend of hers and a fellow Daughter.

The place has ruffledy curtains at the windows and flower boxes outside planted with red geraniums. There's shiny copper pots and stuff and blue plates hanging all over the walls. All they serve is little bitty sandwiches that don't have any taste to them, yucky salads, and soup made out of weird things like watercress and leeks.

Miss Mattie came bustling over to our table wearing one of those Mexican dresses with big old flowers all over it.

"Well, hidy, Mattie," Biggie said. "I just saw that old boyfriend of yours over at the station. Don't know what you see in him. The only ring you'll ever get from him is the one around your bathtub."

Miss Mattie looked around the room to see if anybody heard. Biggie has one of those voices that carries. Finally, she pulled out a chair and took a seat.

"How you, Biggie? How you, J.R.?"

"We're both tolerable," Biggie said. "Did you hear about Crabtree's car?"

"Ooh, yes," Miss Mattie said. "It's being talked all up and down the street. Do they know who did it?"

"Not yet. I expect we'll know soon, though. The chief has one suspect."

Miss Mattie's eyes opened wide. "And . . ."

"Can't say now," Biggie said. "How about a cup of that cranberry tea of yours and a chocolate milk for J.R.?"

When Miss Mattie brought our drinks, Biggie said, "Mattie, has that Norman Thripp told you what the city is up to out on the Plummer place?"

Miss Mattie shook her head.

"Building a garbage dump," Biggie said, "a dang-blasted garbage dump!"

"I wish I'd known you were going out to the farm," Miss Mattie said. "I sure could have used some fresh tomatoes— some of those little cherry types. You going back out there anytime soon?"

Biggie sighed. "I declare, Mattie, sometimes I wonder why I even try to talk to you. Did you hear what I just said?"

"Something about garbage, I think," Miss Mattie said. "By the way, Biggie, folks are already starting to talk about the Pioneer Days festival. Do you have any bright ideas about what we can do this year?"

Biggie gave up. "A few," she said. "Butch over at the flower shop wants to dress up like a mime and do his juggling act during the parade." She picked up her purse and stood up. "Come on, J.R. We've got to get home. Now Mattie, don't you forget, we have called a meeting of the Daughters at my house on Thursday."

When we came out, Butch was sweeping the sidewalk in front of his flower shop. He had on silver tights and a loose white blouse with big sleeves and ruffles that hung down over his hands. Today his hair was dyed pink.

"Hidy, Biggie. Hidy, J.R.," he said. "How do y'all like my new hair color?"

" 'Mornin' Butch," Biggie said. "Your hair looks mighty nice today, but I believe I liked it better when it was chartreuse."

"Do you really?" Butch said. "I'm thinking of dying it yellow for the festival—you know, like the yellow rose of Texas? You should see my mime outfit. I ordered it out of a catalog direct from New Orleans. It's red and white satin with blue sequin stars all over the blouse."

39

"I'm sure you'll be pretty as a field of bluebonnets, Butch," Biggie said, "but we've got to run now. You coming to the planning meeting?"

"Yes'm. Ya'll have a good day, now. You hear?"

5

The day we went to see the mayor, Biggie drove her car right over the sidewalk and parked in front of the mayor's door so he couldn't run away. It's too bad Brother Billy Jack Puckett of the Church of Christ had his little red Toyota parked in the way of where Biggie wanted to go. We sideswiped his car and left a line of black paint all down one side. Biggie got out and took a look at the preacher's car.

"Stars and stripes," she said. "Did I do that?"

Brother Puckett examined the scratch. "It was new," he said almost like he was talking to himself, "my car was brand new. My congregation gave it to me for thirty years of devoted service—never missed a single Sunday. Only missed one Wednesday night prayer meeting, and then only because my wife fell out of a hammock and fractured her scrotum."

"Her *what*?" Biggie said.

Brother Puckett looked at Biggie kind of dazed, like he'd just now noticed her there. "Her scrotum," he said. "You

41

know, that bone in her chest—right between the ribs."

"Oh," said Biggie. "Well, you just send me the bill for the repairs to your car."

The preacher looked up at the sky for a long time. Then he looked down at his shoes. I think he must of been praying. Finally he shook his head. "Oh—that's all right, Miss Biggie. Truth is, I saw you in town twenty minutes ago." He shook his head. "If I'd of had any sense, any sense at all, I'd of gone on home right then and there."

Biggie patted him on the shoulder and told him to bring Mrs. Puckett and come on over for supper real soon.

Dovie, Mayor Gribbons's secretary, who has freckles and large hair, was sitting at her desk reading a paperback book with a picture of a woman in her underwear on the cover. She stuck it in the drawer real fast and smiled up at Biggie.

"Why Miss Biggie Weatherford. How you doin'? Don't tell me your water bill was four cents off again this month?"

"No, my water bill was fine. It's garbage I've come to talk about today. Where's Osbert Gribbons?"

"He's in a real important conference with Mr. Thripp. Is there anything I can help you with? Did Lester forget your pickup again? I swanny, I don't know what we're gonna do with that boy. He ain't worth the lead it'd take to shoot him."

"No, honey. It's not Lester. This is much more important than pickup. I intend to tell Osbert where the cow ate the cabbage!"

"Why don't you come on back in about an hour? They oughta be through by then."

If there's one thing Biggie doesn't like, it's to be kept waiting. I saw the red creeping up around her collar.

"I believe I'll just go in right now. Thank you very much," she said, and walked straight into the mayor's office.

Biggie says the only reason Mayor Gribbons ever got into the business of politics was because they voted the county wet in 1982. She says the Gribbonses had been bootleggers for five generations back. She says bootlegging was all Osbert knew, and the only reason he ran for mayor of Job's Crossing is because that was the only job a miff-minded, jack-legged ex-bootlegger could do around here.

The mayor was talking to Norman Thripp. Neither one looked too overjoyed to see us. Mayor Gribbons smiled his big old catfish smile I guess because he thought he had to on account of Biggie being the richest and most important woman in town. He stood up with a grunt and stuck out his little pink hand for Biggie to shake. Biggie ignored the hand so he used it to run through his silver hair, which he was real proud of. He wore it kind of longish and was fond of saying that someone once told him he looked a little like John Connally.

"Well, if it isn't Mrs. Biggie Weatherford," he said. "How you, ma'am? And I see you've brought young J.R. along. What can we do for you folks today?"

"You can send your equipment out there to cover up that hole your people have dug in the Plummer place. That's what you can do!" Biggie said.

The mayor picked up a pencil off his desk and started twiddling it around his fingers. I guess he was nervous on account of he'd seen that look on Biggie's face before, but he just kept on smiling and looking like he was about to pat her on the head and give her a lollipop.

"Well, Miss Biggie," he said, "that won't be easy. You see, we've already paid the Plummer estate a goodly amount of money to use that land. Our old landfill had outgrown its capacity, don'cha know, due to the fact that the folks down at the box factory dumped a whole year's worth of scraps in there before we here at city hall found out about it." He frowned. "Of course, I spoke sharply to them about it—quite sharply." He reached in his pocket and pulled out a bottle of

43

little white pills and stuck one in his mouth.

"Are you ill, Mayor?" Biggie asked.

"Just the old ticker, Miss Biggie. Doc Hooper's got me taking these pills for my angina. He says I could live to be a hundred if I take care of myself."

I sneaked a peek at his big old belly and wondered if eating everything in sight was his idea of taking care of himself.

Biggie spoke real slow like she does when she wants me to do exactly as she says. "Osbert," she said, "perhaps you are not aware that an important historical cemetery rests on a hill just overlooking that dump."

Norman Thripp looked up from the papers he was reading. "That would be the Wooten graveyard, I suppose," he said, then grinned like a cat eating briars. "Well, heh-heh, we didn't think the folks up there would mind!"

The mayor covered his face with his hand, but I could see he was trying not to laugh.

Biggie saw it, too. "Very well, gentlemen," she said. "We shall see what we shall see! Come on, J.R. We've got work to do."

"Y'all take care, now. You hear?" the mayor called as we went out the door.

I guess those men didn't know that Biggie is a very good person not to mess with. She cooked up a scheme to get rid of that dump, and it was a scheme that few women and no men at all in Job's Crossing would want to try to buck.

"There's nothing that can't be done with teamwork and good common sense," Biggie said. "I'll show that Osbert Gribbons a thing or two!"

The first thing she did was she made up a speech to give to the Daughters at the emergency-called meeting that was to be at our house next week. She made me and Rosebud and Willie Mae listen while she practiced that speech over and over again. It was too long and as boring as an Easter Sunday sermon. I said so but she said if I was a Daughter I wouldn't look at it that way on account of it being all about Pride in Our Heritage and Honoring the Hallowed Ground of Our Forefathers. Then she started back at the first and made us listen to it all over again.

The meeting was to be at our house on Thursday. Biggie made Rosebud work out in the yard all week getting the plants and stuff in tip-top shape.

"Now, Rosebud," she said, "I want you to go down to the feed store and get some of those red and purple petunias they've got in flats out front. Set them out all along the front walk. Get plenty, now. I want it to look like they've been there all summer."

"Miss Biggie, they ain't gonna look like that. They ain't but four inches tall."

"Then go over to city hall and dig some up from around the flagpole."

"I ain't gonna be much good to you when I'm settin' up there in the jailhouse, am I?"

"I guess you're right. I'll tell you what. Go down to Butch's Flower Salon and get some of those potted chrysanthemums, the ones he has for funerals. Get all he's got."

"Yes'm, but them chrysanthemums gonna burn up in this heat."

"I don't care what they do after the meeting. Just go get them."

They went to an awful lot of trouble for a bunch of old ladies that most of them can't see too good anyway.

"I think we'll hold the meeting in the parlor," Biggie said. "Do you think you can have it shipshape by Thursday, Willie Mae?"

" 'Course I can," Willie Mae said, "if all of y'all will stay out of my way while I'm doin' it."

She started right in taking down all the drapes in the living room. She took them out and hung them on the clothes-line and beat them with the broom. It kicked up such a cloud of dust Mrs. Moody thought our house was on fire and called up the fire department.

Biggie greeted Fire Chief Frobisher with a big grin. "Honey," she said, "you boys might just as well hose off the front porch while you're here since you don't have a fire to put out. Just knock the dust off a little. I'm having a mighty important meeting here Thursday—mighty important—and I don't have time to have the house painted."

Chief Frobisher took off his hat and scratched the top of his head. "Great gobs of goose grease, Miss Biggie, we can't do that," he said. "Why, that's against Rule Number Sixty-eight-point-oh-seven of the *City Service Manual:* 'No em-ployee of any city department shall perform any service for any private citizen that shall be construed to be outside the normal activities of said department.' "

"Humph!" Biggie said. "I guess you boys have forgotten the time I bought a brand-new microwave for the fire de-partment after Sparky Lumpkin ruined the old one trying to roast a coon in it."

"Reckon I did, Miss Biggie," the chief said. "Old Sparky forgot that coon was plumb full of buckshot. Shorted the dern thing out."

The firemen got busy and hosed off our porch real good then went around and washed all the windows. I heard one of them say they were hoping for a new popcorn popper.

On Thursday morning we were all sitting down to one of Willie Mae's good breakfasts: scrambled eggs with cheese and popovers with homemade dewberry jam.

Biggie made us listen to her speech all the way through one more time, then said, "Willie Mae, I want you to make some of those little sugar cookies you make so well. Cut them out

46

in the shape of Texas stars, and put a little something in there to make the Daughters receptive to what I have to tell them."

"Miss Biggie, I don't know as I've got anything that'll do that. Not exactly."

"Well, do the best you can."

After breakfast I followed Willie Mae out to her little house.

"Can I watch while you conjure?" I asked.

"Can't nobody watch while I conjure, but you can watch me make up a spell powder," she said.

First she took down some bottles from her little shelf and scrunched up her face as she read the labels. Then, shaking her head, she put each one back.

Next she opened the big cedar chest she keeps at the foot of her bed and started pulling stuff out of there.

"What's in that little red box, Willie Mae?" I asked.

"Look in there and see if you be so nosy," she said.

I looked in there and made a face. "Eeyew! Chicken feet!"

"You always lookin' for something to meddle in," she said, not looking at me. She was examining a jar of something that looked like dried-up leaves. "This here might work. It just might do the trick."

"What is it, Willie Mae? Can I see?"

"Curiosity been known to kill more than cats, boy. You get on back to the house."

I mostly always mind Willie Mae when she uses that tone of voice, but I just had to ask one more question.

"Willie Mae, how did you get to be a voodoo woman? Can I be a voodoo man when I grow up?"

Now she was looking at a red Chinese jar filled with some white and pink crystals. She gave me a look that told me I'd better get out of there. I went and sat on the steps. Booger came and sat on my lap. We waited for a long time but she never came out. I couldn't be sure, but I thought I heard singing coming from the little house. Finally, I got bored and went to find Biggie. That was a mistake because she made me vacuum the living room rug.

Next, she made me polish her mama's silver tea service, which wasn't too bad because, after I finished, I went out and rubbed my black hands all over Mrs. Moody's little white dog, Prissy. I made him striped.

When I got back in, Willie Mae was baking cookies. They smelled good and I asked for just one, but Willie Mae told me to get in that bathtub and to not come out until I was clean and that meant my fingernails, too. Then she made me put on clean clothes and go out on the front porch to wait for the ladies to arrive.

6

I was sitting on the front steps playing with my baby duck, Donald, when the Daughters started arriving.

Miss Lonie Fulkerson, who is tongue-tied and also very nosy, was the first one up the steps. Biggie says if you want anything broadcast all over town, don't put it in the paper, tell Lonie—she'll get the job done and it won't cost you a cent. Miss Lonie's hair is blue like a Brillo pad and from the looks of it, it more than likely feels like one, too. Today she had it covered up with a big red straw hat that matched her dress, which was red with black roses all over it.

"Hello, Jameth Royth," she said. "How ith your mothah? Doth she have a thweetheart?"

"No, ma'am. She has a Plymouth."

"Hee! Hee! Jameth Royth. What a thtrange little boy you are."

"Yes, ma'am."

Next came Miss Mattie McClure and Mrs. Estelle Scroggins, whose husband owns Scroggins Lumberyard. Once he gave me a rope to make a swing absolutely free on account of it was the end of the spool and nobody else was going to buy a piece of rope that short. I like Mrs. Scroggins. She works in the store with Mr. Scroggins. Miss Mattie giggles a lot and keeps taking a compact out of her purse and looking at herself in it. I don't know why she wants to do that since she has no chin and a nose like a macaw. I heard Biggie tell Willie Mae that Mattie McClure was going to get Norman Thripp to marry her if it hare-lipped the governor.

"Hidy, J.R.," Mrs. Scroggins said. "If you'll come down to the store tomorrow, I'll give you some end pieces of lumber we've got out back. You can make you a tree house."

"Or a spaceship!" I said. "Thanks!"

Next came Mrs. Vestal Chapman, who walks with crutches on account of breaking her hip and it not healing right.

Just as she came up the steps, Donald jumped out of my lap and ran under a crutch. He was sure lucky. That crutch just barely missed his head. It landed on his foot and smashed it right off. Now, when he swims, he only goes in circles.

After that, a whole carload of Daughters arrived. I only recognized two of them. One was Mrs. Ruby Muckleroy, the only woman in town as rich as Biggie. She's a descendant by marriage of Eleanor Ann Muckleroy that married old James Royce. She's got freckles all over her face and all over her arms. She was wearing a big straw hat with bluebonnets around the brim. The other lady I knew was Miss Emily Crews, who was my second-grade teacher and is very skinny with the longest, narrowest feet I have ever seen. She has to send off to Chicago for her shoes. She told Biggie they cost so much money she can only afford to buy two pairs a year.

As they were going in, I heard Mrs. Muckleroy say, "I hope Biggie's cleaned up the house. The last time we met here I got hay fever from all that dust."

I guess she thinks I'm deaf or something.

The last to arrive was Miss Julia Lockhart, who writes a column for the paper, "Job's Jottings from Julia." Biggie said she could be a big help in the campaign.

Since there wasn't anything better to do, I sat on the porch swing and listened to the meeting.

Biggie let them visit and have refreshments before she made them listen to her speech. They sounded just exactly like the chickens out at Monica's farm.

"Did you hear about poor Mrs. Lumpkin?"

"What'd the doctor find out?"

"Honey, she was eat up with cancer. They just sewed her back up and sent her home. So sad . . ."

"I wonder what poor Mr. Lumpkin will do, a widower and all." That was Miss Julia. "I might just bake a cake and take it over to him. How long you think she's got?"

"Not long, I imagine," Mrs. Muckleroy said. "I know when Theodore's brother had it, he went fast. He always said he wanted it that way. Never wanted to linger and be a burden on his people."

"That's the way I want to go, too."

"Me too."

"Don't any of us know when the Lord's gonna call us home."

"Did any of y'all hear what happened to Bernice Glick last weekend?" Mrs. Muckleroy asked.

"No, honey. What did?" someone said.

"Well, I wouldn't tell it on her if she didn't act so stuck-up all the time."

"That's the Yankee in her, honey. You know her mama came from Iowa, or one of them places."

"You'd think she was Mrs. God or something."

"Well, listen, won't you," Mrs. Muckleroy said. "Bernice and Tuck (that's her *third* husband) went to Bossier City to

51

one of them casinos they've got over there. Well, when they came back, they had to sell their car. That Tuck had lost every single dime they had to their name—playin' roulette. I guess Bernice won't be so stuck-up riding around town in Tuck's wrecker truck!"

"Poor Bernith," said Miss Lonie. "I wonder how much they got for that car. It wathent anything but jutht an old 'eighty-one Ithu-thu."

"Mattie, what have you done with your hair? It looks downright silky."

"Itha's got in this highfalutin new conditioner stuff over at the shop. It's made with the same stuff they put on horses' manes to get them to shine. You can't get it in the grocery store—they'll only sell it through beauty salons."

"Well, I may get me some. You think it'll work on this old frizzy stuff of mine?"

"You could try it."

"How much does it cost? A lot, I'll bet. Biggie, I believe I'll just have one more of those delicious cookies."

"Good idea. Pass them over this way."

"I've got to get Willie Mae's recipe for these—"

"Me too! Um-um, they are mighty tasty."

"Have a little more tea," Biggie said. She was pouring out of her mama's silver pot into her china teacups with the family crest printed in gold on the sides. Biggie's family crest is a mailed fist holding up a wild boar's head. After everybody'd had more tea and a few more cookies, Biggie got up and commenced to talk. It was the same boring speech she'd made me and Willie Mae listen to. But the Daughters liked it a lot. Pretty soon they started in clapping and stomping their feet and saying, "Tell um, Biggie!" and "Amen, sister," which I thought was a pretty strange way for a bunch of old ladies to act. I wondered if Willie Mae had put the wrong spell in those cookies.

Biggie was just getting warmed up.

"Fellow Daughters, evil lurks at our very doorstep. Those devils at city hall have put garbage—yes, I say *garbage*—on the very ground where our forefathers first set foot on this hallowed portion of God's green earth known as Kemp County, Texas!"

"Oh no!" the Daughters all hollered.

"Its noxious runoff will bespoil the crystal-clear waters of Wooten Creek!"

"That's right!" they answered, clapping their hands.

"Its fetid stench will foul our pure air!"

"Never!" they yelled, stomping their feet.

"We must stop them before it's too late!" Biggie shouted. "Hold Our Ground!"

"Hold Our Ground!" the Daughters yelled. "Hold Our Ground! Hold Our Ground!"

After that, Biggie got them calmed down enough to repeat the Daughters' Creed, and they all left to go down to city hall to give the mayor what for.

Mrs. Muckleroy's hat was tilted way over to one side and a bluebonnet was hanging down over one eye. Vestal Chapman was walking as good as anybody, carrying her crutch over her shoulder like a rifle.

I jumped on my bike and followed them down to the town square. As it turned out, the mayor and Chief Trotter had gone fishing, so they all joined hands around the statue of James Royce and sang three choruses of "Texas, Our Texas, All Hail Thee, Mighty State." A pretty good crowd had gathered by then, so Biggie stood on a park bench and gave her speech all over again. Then the Daughters all marched back to their cars shouting "Hold Our Ground!"

Later, when I was helping Willie Mae clean up the mess, I said, "Willie Mae, what kind of spell did you put in those cookies?"

"I'll tell you a secret, J.R., if you promise not to tell a soul."

"I won't tell. See, I'm zipping my lips up tight."

"Well, I didn't exactly have what you might call a protest spell so I used the same one I made up for a preacher once to use at a revival meeting."

The very next day, Miss Lockhart got the paper to print up bumper stickers for all the Daughters' cars that said H.O.G. for "Hold Our Ground."

Judge Franklin Delano Grimes is our county judge and he's sweet on Biggie. I think it's pretty disgusting for a person so old to be thinking that way. The morning after the meeting, he called Biggie up and invited her to have lunch with him and bring me along. I was busy, but Biggie made me go anyway.

We drove out to the Catfish Cabin on the lake. I like the Catfish Cabin. It's a huge log cabin set in a big grove of pine trees. They have a boat dock and a pier where you can look down into the clear water and see the fishes swimming around.

"Biggie, can I go out on the pier?" I asked.

"After we eat, honey. First I want you to promise me you'll be polite to the judge when he comes—oh, there he is now."

The judge has wavy white hair and always wears a black suit and a string tie. Biggie says he's very distinguished looking. I think he looks like Grandpa Walton.

Judge Grimes took off his hat and bowed to Biggie. "What an honor and a privilege it is to be having lunch with two of my favorite people," he said.

I could of sworn Biggie blushed.

Just then the waitress come to take our order.

"Pitch 'til you win all around," the judge said.

I was beginning to like him better already. Biggie never lets me order anything more than the regular dinner even though she knows I can eat more catfish than anybody in town except for maybe the mayor.

While we were waiting for the fish, they brought out a big basket of hush puppies and some green-tomato relish, which we dived right into on account of it's almost as good as the fish themselves.

"Franklin," Biggie said (if I didn't know her better, I'd think she was batting her eyelashes), "have you heard anything about anyone leasing for lignite in this county?"

"Matter of fact, I have," he said, "and I don't mind telling you, I'm upset about it. I grew up in West Virginia, as you know, and I know what strip-mining can do to the land."

"Do you know of anyone that's already leased?" she asked.

"I'm sorry to say, some of your neighbors out at the farm have already signed, and others are giving it serious thought." He shook his head. "Frankly, Biggie, there's not much can be done about it if a landowner is willing to lease—and the money's damn good. What's this I hear about you and the other Daughters protesting the new dump?"

Biggie's eyes lit up and she sat up straighter. "Never underestimate the power of a determined group of women," she said. "Already that dump is doomed. You mark my words."

"Is there anything I can do to help?"

"Do you have any influence with the city?"

"Not so you could tell it. You know how Gribbons and Thripp are. They play it close to the vest. Personally, I think those two would steal flowers off their own grandmother's grave, and I'll bet my hat they're aiming to make some money out of that coal-mining operation."

The fish came, a great big platter just piled high with whole fried catfish still sizzling from the pan. I was on my third one when I slowed up enough to pay attention to the fact that they were talking about mining again.

"Well, I'm not giving up," Biggie was saying. "There's just bound to be something we can do—and I aim to find it."

"To tell the truth, Biggie," the judge said, "I figure you've got about as much chance as a runaway turkey in downtown Dallas to stop them now. If I was you I'd concentrate on getting rid of the dump and forget about the mining. Still, this might help. Why don't I get Jimmie Sue to run the records and find out if anybody's already signed leases. They'd be filed in the county clerk's office. Then you and the other Daughters can contact the neighboring landowners and try to stop it going any farther."

"Good!" Biggie said, spearing the biggest catfish on the plate. "Maybe you ought to have the waitress bring out another platter."

"What? Oh, catfish," the judge said, and laughed. "Nettie Ruth! Another platter over here."

After we finished, Biggie let me go down to the pier while they had coffee. Then we went home, and Biggie was in a good mood all day.

7

One thing I like to do is dig around in the old records at the courthouse. I guess I like that so much on account of my great-granddaddy, Eldridge Semple Wooten, who was a lawyer and an abstract man. I must have it in my blood because I even like the way the courthouse smells. Biggie says maybe I'm going to be a historian when I grow up and can write a book about James Royce. She keeps forgetting I'm going to be a space ranger. Anyway, that's why I wasn't too upset when she told me I had to go with her to the planning-committee meeting for Pioneer Days.

"The meeting's in the courthouse basement," Biggie said while she powdered her nose. "You can mess around in those old record books they have stored down there while we take care of business."

As it turned out, I was glad I went even though I missed a science fiction festival on Channel Eight. It was one of the most exciting nights of my whole life. I would have missed the whole thing if it hadn't of been Wednesday night, which is the night Willie Mae goes to choir practice at Saint Thelma's CME Church and couldn't stay home and take care of me. She made Rosebud go too, even though he said he didn't think the pope would approve, him being Catholic and all. Willie Mae said the pope needed all the help he could get where Rosebud was concerned, even Methodist help, and anyway, he had to go because Louie Ray Jefferson was down with a cold and they needed a good strong bass.

"I didn't know you could sing, Rosebud," I said.

"Like a bird, son, like a bird. Did I ever tell you about the time I was all set to sing 'Old Man River' in the New Orleans Light Opera production of *Showboat*?"

"Uh-uh."

"It was a sad thing. An unfortunate case of mistaken identity landed me in the parish jail on opening night. The show closed after only two performances due to my unforeseen incarceration."

"Hurry up, J.R.," Biggie called from her bedroom, "and get me my umbrella out of the hall closet. It looks like rain."

"Biggie," I said on the way over, "do you think the old deed to your farm is down there in those old records?"

"It wasn't a deed, honey," she said. "It was a land grant and, yes, I imagine it's in there somewhere. You know, James Royce came here before Texas was even a state."

She parked the car in the space marked off for the sheriff and said, "Hurry up, J.R. It's going to be a gully washer."

Just then a big old clap of thunder came and we scooted into the building. At the door we met Chief Trotter and Jimmie Sue, who had on a yellow sundress and looked pretty as one of Willie Mae's lemon pies.

"Found out anything, Chief?" Biggie asked.

"No ma'am. That biker feller seems to have left town. At

least I can't find him. He was staying out at the motel but Raymond, the clerk, says he checked out last Tuesday."

"Thank goodness," Jimmie Sue said. "He's a real slimeball (pardon the expression, Miss Biggie), and I hope he don't never come back. Creepy, is what he was."

"I think you're going to have to find a motive, Chief," Biggie said. "Someone must have had a reason to want to hurt poor Mr. Crabtree."

"Yes'm. I'll keep you posted," the chief said.

Most everybody had already taken seats around the table when we got to the meeting room. Miss Mattie McClure and Norman Thripp were together at one end, her looking like she'd just roped the biggest steer at the rodeo and him not looking at her at all but talking up a blue streak to Bertram Handy, who runs the feed store on back street.

The most important Daughters were there, along with most of the people who owned businesses around the square. Mayor Gribbons was seated at the head of the table holding the gavel. Biggie walked over and took it out of his hand and stood behind the podium.

"As chairperson of the Pioneer Days Steering Committee, I now call the meeting to order," she said. "As you all know, this meeting is for the purpose of planning the most important event of our year. The date has been set for the first weekend in October." She stopped talking and looked at Miss Lonie Fulkerson, who had started in painting her nails. Miss Lonie put the nail polish back in her purse. Biggie continued. "The proceeds will be used to repair the gazebo at the city park which was shot full of holes when Arvil Simpson took one of his spells and thought the Russians were coming."

Biggie had to pound her gavel a few times because Jimmie Sue, who was supposed to be taking the minutes, was whispering a joke to George M. Oterwald, who owns the hardware store. Biggie gave her a look and she picked up her pencil and started in writing.

"The chair now opens the floor for suggestions," Biggie said.

The mayor stood up. "Ladies and gentlemen," he said. "As your mayor, I have prepared a patriotic speech, which I plan to give in the park as soon as the parade is over. I shall speak of the glories of our town, both past and present. For, as you know, since I have been in office, we have brought about numerous benefits for our citizens—"

"Like what," Mr. Handy said, "the potholes in the streets or the fact that the trash don't get picked up mor'n oncet ever two or three weeks?"

"I was referring to the renovations to the city hall," the mayor said. "There ain't a town in east Texas that's got a more elegant city hall than we got right here in our fair city."

Biggie pounded the gavel and Mrs. Muckleroy raised her hand.

"Ruby," Biggie said.

"I propose a charity ball for Saturday night," she said. "Black tie. We could use the VFW hall and charge twenty-five dollars for tickets."

The ladies, all but Biggie, clapped their hands.

"Ooh!" Miss Mattie said, "We could decorate the whole place like a winter wonderland—with snowflakes and silver icicles! I've always wanted to go to a winter wonderland ball ever since my cousin Bernice, who lives in Detroit, told me about one she went to. All the women wore white and the men wore black tuxedos. Bernice said it was just the prettiest thing she'd ever seen in her whole life."

"That might be just fine for Detroit," said Mrs. Moody, "but this here's Texas. Maybe we could have a spring fantasy, with flowers and birds all over the place. . . ."

"I'll do the decorating—at cost!" said Butch.

"It's going to be in October, Essie! Use your head," Miss Mattie said.

"Oh yeah, I forgot," Mrs. Moody said.

"How about an evening in Paris?" Miss Julia Lockhart suggested. "So romantic!"

"Or 'Thtairway to the Thtars,' " said Miss Lonie Fulkerson.

"I could decorate that, too," Butch said. "I'd use lots of dark blue crepe paper and silver stars all around. Ooh—and we could have one of those mirror balls revolving in the center of the room."

Biggie slammed down her gavel.

"Ladies, please! Remember, this is Pioneer Days we're planning, not a coming-out party. Still—a dance might not be such a bad idea. How about a barn dance? We could decorate the hall with bales of hay and red-checked tablecloths. I'm sure we can get Hooter Davis and his Jug Band Five to play for us. The chair calls for a vote. All in favor of a barn dance say 'Aye.' "

Biggie's idea passed because the men, all except Butch, voted with her so they wouldn't have to get all dressed up.

"The chair recognizes the chairman of the Rodeo Committee," Biggie said.

Chief Trotter stood up.

"All sewed up, Miss Biggie," he said. "The Famous Bronco Busters of Casper Wyoming will be here. They have animals, clowns, cowboys . . . the works! And this year we have a big surprise. We have arranged for the Clem Clawson Shows, a carnival, to be here . . . Ferris wheel and all!"

Everyone clapped.

"Will there be cotton candy?" asked the mayor. "I sure do love cotton candy."

"Most likely," said the chief, who didn't know any better than me if there'd be cotton candy but was happy to stay in

the limelight as long as possible. "Candy apples, too, probably—and foot-long hot dogs. They always have foot-long
hot dogs."

"Thank you, Chief. Now we'll hear from the Parade Com-
mittee, of which I am the chairperson. As of now, we have
promises of floats from the Rotary Club, the Ladies' Study
Club, the Four-H, the Future Farmers of America, and the
Women's Quilting Society. I'm waiting to hear from the Boy
Scouts and the Girl Scouts.

"The Mooslah Temple of Texarkana has agreed to come
and bring their darling little cars again this year. I have asked
them not to blow their horns or throw any stink bombs on
the pavement. I'm sure you all remember the unfortunate in-
cident two years ago when they stampeded the horses and
tore down the cute-baby-contest display."

"I remember," said the chief. "I had to keep most of um
overnight in jail that year."

"And, finally," Biggie continued, "we will have several
area high-school bands as well as our local beauty queens
riding in open cars."

Everyone clapped and smiled except Mrs. Muckleroy, who
was still pouting over not getting to have a ball.

Biggie raised her hand.

"This year, as usual, I have requested that everyone dress
in old-timey clothes—so go to your attic and drag out
Grandma's old wardrobe. Let's make this year's celebration
a real barn burner!"

The meeting went on and on, so I went back in the shelves
and started looking through the old record books. I did find
the land grant to James Royce Wooten, and I also found
something else—something I didn't exactly understand. But
in the excitement of all that happened that night, I forgot to
tell Biggie about it until much later.

By the time I came out, the meeting was breaking up.

Everybody stood out in the hall talking and waiting for the rain to slack off. It was going to be the best festival ever; everybody pretty much agreed on that. The question of whether a barn dance was the best thing was being whispered about by some of the Daughters standing over to one side, but no one was brave enough to argue with Biggie about it. The chief and Jimmie Sue thought a carnival was a good thing, but Norman Thripp wasn't too sure because it would take money away from the local booths and attractions. Miss Mattie asked if the folks that worked there would be all dirty and have tattoos and try to flirt with the young girls. Miss Julie Lockhart, whose sister had run off with the circus in 'fifty-eight, said they'd probably all be gypsies and the ladies would have to watch their purses *and* their children. Biggie said, in a firm voice, that that was nonsense and that there hadn't been any gypsies around here since she was a girl. Jimmie Sue said she didn't care if they had foot-long hot dogs or not, the B.&P.W. was still going to run their hot-dog booth just like always. Butch said for a barn dance he'd use white daisies in little blue tin pitchers on all the tables and drape the bandstand with blue denim tied up with red bandannas.

Just then the judge, who'd been working late, came out of his office.

"Ah-ha," he said. "I see the movers and shakers of this town have completed their mission."

"That's right, Delano," the mayor said. "And since you were conspicuous by your absence, we have elected you chair of the Horse Manure Shoveling Committee."

"Well, I don't know about that, Osbert," the judge said. "I heard a feller say if horse manure was music, you'd be a whole symphony orchestra. How about we reconvene this meeting over at the café over coffee and dessert?"

"Can we, Biggie?" I asked.

"Don't see why not," Biggie said. "All that presiding's left me dry as the middle of a haystack."

So we all headed over to the cafe, except for Jimmie Sue, who made the chief take her home on account of she said all that rain was giving her an asthma attack.

8

Mr. Popolus looks like his face caught fire and somebody put it out with a hammer. His hair is gray and curly and sticks straight up like a wire brush. He runs the Owl Cafe. I think he must be a nice man because he always feeds Ralph, the town dog, with scraps from the kitchen. Everybody in Job's Crossing says he makes the best desserts in Texas. We have a sign out by the city limits that says: JOB'S CROSSING, FRIENDLIEST TOWN THIS SIDE OF THE RED RIVER—HOME OF POPOLUS'S PIES! Mr. Popolus gets lots of business, especially when court is in session, on account of his café being right across the street from the courthouse.

Biggie went right straight to the big round table in the middle of the room and sat down, motioning for me to sit on her right and the judge to sit on her left.

"Come on over here, you three," she called out to Miss Lonie and Miss Mattie and Norman Thripp. "This table's bigger than Brewster County. You too, Mayor. Take a seat over here."

The mayor came and sat down with a big old grunt. He turned to me and smiled like a dead hog in the sunshine.

"What'll you have, son?" he asked, messing up my hair with his little pink hand. "Anything, so long's it don't cost more'n a dime."

I thought he'd bust a gut laughing at his own joke.

"What do you want, honey?" Biggie asked. "I'm just going to have a cup of coffee, myself."

"Ice cream with chocolate syrup," I said. "What happened to the chief and Jimmie Sue?"

"Jimmie Thue thtarted having an athma attack," Miss Lonie said, "tho the chief took her home. You thould of heard her. Wheething to beat the band!"

"What kind of pies you got tonight, Popolus?" asked Mr. Thripp.

"Chocolate, lemon, cherry, *opple* and *peenopple*," Mr. Popolus said. Mr. Popolus talks funny on account of being from Greece.

"I'll take *peenopple*," Mr. Thripp said, grinning and poking the mayor with his elbow.

He quit when Biggie looked at him.

The mayor said, "I'm hungry enough to eat the south end of a north-bound skunk. You know what I always order, Popolus."

"Some nice angel food cake," Mr. Popolus said, "with whipped cream on top."

"Yessirree! That's for me," said the mayor, "and throw a few fresh strawberries on there if you got um."

"And while you're enjoying it, you might just give some thought to where you're going to move that dump you people have put out on the Plummer place," said Mrs. Muckleroy, who was sitting at the next table with Butch and Mr. and Mrs. Oterwald.

"Now, Ruby," said Biggie, patting the mayor on the hand, "I'm sure Mayor Gribbons and Mr. Thripp have already done that. Am I right, gentlemen?"

"Well, you know, Miss Biggie, we already told you we can't move the new landfill."

There was a murmur among the other Daughters that sounded like a nest of hornets. Mr. Thripp took out his handkerchief and wiped off his bald head.

"Of course you can, honey," said Biggie. "Why not put it on your grandpa's place. It's nothing but marshland, anyway—nothing'll grow there but switch cane and grapevines. Since your grandpa made his living making whiskey, he didn't have to worry too much about the soil."

The mayor looked like lightning just struck his zipper but, I got to hand it to him, he kept on smiling.

"Never mind," Biggie said. "Here comes our food. Let's just all enjoy ourselves for tonight. I'm sure the mayor and Mr. Thripp will think of something."

Just then the big glass door with a picture of an owl etched on it opened and the chief came in. He took a seat at the counter.

"What's the matter, Chief," the mayor hollered, "little lady wouldn't give you any sugar tonight?"

The chief looked around for a hole to hide in and didn't find one. "She ain't feelin' too good," he said.

Mr. Popolus came out of the kitchen carrying a big tray. After he'd passed out all the food, he said, "Almost closing time. Popolus will be in the kitchen. Yell if you need him."

I was just digging into my ice cream when I saw the mayor take out his little bottle of pills and pop one into his mouth. His eyes were open wide and he'd turned blue.

"Biggie—" I said.

At that moment, Mayor Gribbons made a little hissing sound, like a fart, and grabbed his throat with both hands.

Biggie patted him on the back. "Honey, are you all right? Are you choking?"

By now, he had turned almost as black as Rosebud and was taking deep breaths. His face looked like Arl the Mole King. Sometimes, when I can't go to sleep at night, I remember that face and the way his eyes seemed to be staring right at Biggie, like he was trying to tell her something.

"Somebody, help!" Mrs. Muckleroy hollered. "He's choking!"

The mayor's head all of a sudden just dropped right down into his plate of cake and whipped cream. Biggie grabbed him by the hair and pulled his head up. He sure looked silly with strawberries and whipped cream all over his face. He didn't care though, I don't guess, seeing as he was already dead.

The folks all stood around jabbering away at each other and not doing anything until Biggie said, "Lonie, you go call Doctor Hooper. Tell him to get over here. Fast! J.R., you go in the kitchen and get me a clean towel."

I ran in the kitchen just as Mr. Popolus was coming in from feeding Ralph. I told him what had happened and he ran out and handed Biggie a clean towel.

She wiped the mayor's face cleaner than was necessary to my way of thinking since the undertaker would probably hose him down good, then she stuck the towel in her big black purse.

"Biggie," I said, "you're taking—"

"Shh! Go sit at the counter and finish your ice cream."

I went and sat down, but I wasn't hungry anymore. I'd seen dead things before. Once I had a cat that ate a poisoned mouse and died right under my bed. Another time, Daddy took me on a hunting trip. We got four squirrels and made stew out of them right there in the woods. But this was a whole 'nother kettle of fish. The mayor was a human being, and he'd been sitting right there at the table with us no more than five minutes ago just being his same old obnoxious self then, quicker than a hiccup, he's dead in his dessert.

By this time everybody had moved over by the door, as far away from the body as they could get. One thing was sure, Mayor Gribbons was a goner. What killed him was the thing nobody could agree on. Mrs. Muckleroy said he always was too fat, even as a boy, so it was probably his heart, but Mr. Oterwald wasn't convinced because he said the Gribbonses were all fat and old Grandpa Gribbons lived to be a hundred and two and they had to bury him in a piano crate. Someone said they ought to notify his brother out in Phoenix, but the judge said he doubted it would do much good on account of they hadn't spoken in twenty-five years. Biggie pulled a plastic tablecloth off the next table and spread it over the mayor, then stuck her head under there with him for a few seconds. It happened so quick I didn't think anyone but me noticed. Then I saw someone watching with a look that reminded me of Mim, King of the Plutonians, when he was about to zap Commander Corey into the Ovens of Planetary Doom.

Dr. Hooper came shuffling into the café carrying his black bag. Dr. Hooper is what Biggie calls a "rubbing doctor," which means he's not a real doctor. He's all we've got in Job's Crossing, though. Most folks, when they're serious about medical treatment, go over to Center Point for care where they've got two osteopaths, a dentist, and a vet. Dr. Hooper went right to work on the mayor.

"Heart attack," said the doctor after he'd finished poking around on the body. "The mayor here had a mighty bad heart."

Biggie snorted.

"Mighty bad heart," Dr. Hooper said, "diseased, as a matter of fact. The man had a diseased heart!"

"Still and all," Biggie said, "when a man just falls over dead in his cake like the mayor just did, it seems to me like you might ought to send him over to Tyler for an autopsy, Travis."

"That's right," Mrs. Muckleroy said. "You can't be too careful."

"Oo-wee," said Miss Mattie. "I seen a TV show once about autopsies. You should see what they do to those bodies. It ain't Christian."

"It ain't Christian to let a murderer get away with it, either," said Biggie. "I think you should order an autopsy, Chief. And as county judge, Franklin, you can act as medical examiner, seeing as this county has no justice of the peace."

"If you think so, Miss Biggie," said the chief. "Now, somebody call Smitt's Funeral Home and have them send the hearse over here. They can hold him until morning."

"Do what you like, Chief," said Dr. Hooper, "but this man had a dis-eased heart!"

The rain had stopped when we stepped outside, and a full moon was shining through the trees around the courthouse square. Ralph was out back barking his head off.

"J.R., run back there and see what that dog's barking at," Biggie said.

I went around in the alley. It was dark back there and damp and spooky. Just as I rounded the corner of the building, I thought I heard someone running down the alley. Ralph stopped barking and ran up to me, wagging his tail. I patted him on the head and, when I did, I saw something shiny on the ground. I picked it up and wiped it on my pants. When I saw what it was, I got out of there fast. It was another silver concho just like the one I'd found in our front yard. I gave it to Biggie as soon as we got home.

When I got back to the front of the café, everybody had left but Biggie and the chief.

"What do you think killed him, Chief?" Biggie asked.

"I don't know, Miss Biggie. It seems mighty strange, don't it? The mayor falling over, dead as a sardine, in his dessert like that."

"I'm of the same opinion, Chief. Something didn't smell right to me."

The next day, Biggie woke me up early and made me and Rosebud go out behind the café and look for clues.

"How will I know a clue if I see one, Biggie?"

"You'll know. Just bring back anything that looks, you know, interesting."

"I'll know, Miss Biggie. Did I ever tell you about the time I captured Knucklebones Thibadeaux, the meanest crook in Saint Martinville Parish, single-handed? They gave me a—"

"Later, Rosebud," Biggie said. "You've got to get down there before all the sightseers start poking around and stepping all over the evidence. Hurry!"

The alley was still damp from last night's rain and smelled like all the garbage that ever was. It looked like Ralph had made him a nest back there. I saw an old blanket shoved up under a packing crate along with several bones, Ralph's bowl with leftover dessert from last night, and a chewed-up woman's shoe. I picked it up and looked inside. It was a size eight. Ralph wasn't home.

Rosebud kept walking up and down the alley, picking up stuff and then throwing it back on the ground. Then he happened to see Opal Mae Mosley, who cooks for Mr. Popolus, standing at the kitchen door.

"Whatchall doin' out there?" she asked.

Rosebud started in telling her about the time he was a detective for the Baton Rouge police force. I kept on looking. I found an old leather hatband, black, which I thought might make a collar for Booger, and some broken glass. I started picking up the pieces of glass and putting them in the sack Biggie had given me for collecting clues. I found several suspicious-looking rocks, so I collected them along with a rusty nail and a bottle cap from a Grapette, which might be valuable. Just then I heard Rosebud say, "We gotta be goin' now. Lots of detecting to do. Miss Biggie depends on me, you know."

"Rosebud," I said, "look what I found."

"What? That old broken glass? Come on, boy. We gotta go. Next thing I know, you'll be collecting dirt."

I took the sack home and gave it to Biggie and she put it in her dresser drawer. "Go get washed up," she said. "It's lunchtime."

9

"J.R.," Biggie said the next day, "I have to go over to Lonie's house and, while I'm gone, I want you and Rosebud to paint the back fence."

"Yes'm," I said. "How come you're going over there?"

"I've called a special meeting of the Daughters," she said. "We're fixing to make signs to carry and banners to wear in the Pioneer Days parade—protesting the new dump, don'cha know." She picked up her purse then put it back down. "Willie Mae," she called, "you in there?"

Willie Mae came out of the kitchen wiping her hands on a dish towel. "Yes'm," she said.

"You seen Crabtree?"

"Yes'm. He's settin' right in my kitchen eatin' eggs."

"Would you mind telling him to come in here for just a minute?"

"No'm."

Mr. Crabtree came hotfootin' it out of the kitchen wiping his hands on a towel. "Miss Biggie," he said, putting the towel down on the back of the sofa, "you look fine as the bonny blue flag in that dress. Where might you be off to this lovely morning?"

"No rest for the weary," Biggie said. "I've a million things to do, but I have something for you that you're gonna just love to death. J.R., go get me that cap I bought at that flea market in Lufkin. It's on the floor in my closet."

When I reached down to get it off the floor, it slapped me on account of it wasn't the cap at all. It was Booger. He'd made himself a bed inside that cap. I'd picked him up by the tail by mistake.

"Looky here, honey," Biggie said, holding up the cap. "You're going to get to wear this in the parade along with Grandpa Wooten's World War One uniform. Try it on!"

The big smile Mr. Crabtree had been wearing kind of melted off his face. "That?" he said.

"Sure, honey," Biggie said, "you'll look downright dashing in it."

There's one thing about Mr. Crabtree. He knows when he's licked. He took the cap from her and put it on his head. Just as he did, a flea hopped out and landed on his nose.

"Help!" he said, slapping himself on the face. "My stars, what was that?"

The flea hopped back into the cap.

"Never mind, honey," Biggie said, taking the cap from his head. "I'll dust it good with flea powder before the parade. Now, you'll be riding with J.R. and Monica in the farm wagon. Rosebud will drive wearing his Mardi Gras costume, which he tells me is of an Indian chief." She held the cap up by the tail. "J.R.," she said, "go outside and hang this thing on the fence in the sun. It does seem to have a slight odor to it."

While I was helping Rosebud paint the back fence, he told me about the time he painted the governor's mansion in

Baton Rouge single-handed, and the governor came out and personally handed him a hundred-dollar bill because he was doing such a good job.

Mr. Crabtree was sitting under the crape myrtle drinking a glass of tea and working on his book about the pope. He glanced up from his book. "Rosebud," he said, "you should be ashamed of yourself for telling this innocent child such bald-faced lies."

Rosebud just grinned and said he recollected the time he bet a feller he could drink four milk shakes in fifteen minutes and the feller disbelieved him and put twenty dollars on the table that said he couldn't. Rosebud said he managed to do it but his tongue froze and stuck to his teeth and the doctor had to remove part of his tongue to get it loose. He said he'd do it again just to show me and I didn't even have to put up the twenty dollars.

I didn't believe it, but if he was willing to take the chance of getting his tongue frozen to his teeth again, I sure didn't want to miss it. I went and got the money out of my bank and rode my bike down to the Eazee Freeze, which is all the way through town and clear to the end of Atlanta Street. It's just a little old frame building, not much too look at, but Job's Crossing folks know Mr. Peoples, who runs it, makes his hamburgers with real meat and uses tomatoes he grows right out back of the building. He does right smart more business than the big chains out on the bypass. I could of gone to the drugstore, which is closer, but I happen to know Mr. Peoples gives double milk shakes on Saturday to get you in there so you'll order a hamburger and fries to go with it.

Mr. Peoples used to rodeo and always wears a cowboy hat to work and chaps and boots under his apron. He sometimes plays his guitar and sings for the customers on Saturday night. He only knows two songs, "Ghost Riders in the Sky," and "Mule Train," but that don't matter. He'll just sing one first then sing the other for an encore. Biggie says he'd be a rich man if he'd just lose that guitar. She says no hamburger's good enough to listen to Aubrey Peoples sing those same two songs over and over. She once tried to teach him "When It's Roundup Time in Texas," but he said that wasn't lively enough and, if she didn't mind, he'd just stick with what he knew.

"Howdy, J.R.," said Mr. Peoples when I walked in. "Hear you were present when the mayor headed for the last roundup."

"Huh?"

"Died, son. When he died."

"Oh. Yes, sir. He fell right over in his cake and whipped cream. I need four chocolate milk shakes and a limeade to drink while you make them."

"Hungry enough to eat a saddle blanket after a day's ridin', are you?"

"No, sir. It's not for me. They're all for Rosebud. You ever see one man drink four milk shakes?"

"I ain't never seen one *hombre* drink *two* of my milk shakes, buckaroo. They're good, but mighty fillin'. Chocolate, you say?"

"Yes, sir."

I was just slurping up the last of my limeade when somebody sat down on the stool next to mine. I glanced around and what I saw gave me goose bumps as big as nickels. It was the biker—sitting so close to me I could smell him. The funny thing was, he didn't smell like sweat and leather at all, like I would of expected. He smelled like the stuff Mama used to put on before she'd go out. White Shoulders, I think she called it.

He didn't look at me, just ordered the special, which was a steak-finger basket.

"Here you go, pardner," Mr. Peoples said, shoving my milk shakes at me. "That'll be four ninety-five."

I laid the money on the counter and started to leave just as the biker reached for the catsup. That's when I got the surprise of my life. He had a big tattoo on his arm, which is not so surprising seeing as he was a biker and all. But that particular tattoo was a mailed fist holding up a boar's head, which is Biggie's family crest. Then things got really weird. He asked Mr. Peoples if he knew Mrs. Fiona Wooten Weatherford. Biggie!

I grabbed my milk shakes and got out of there before Mr. Peoples could tell him who I was. You don't want to mess with those bikers. They kidnap little children and give them drugs and make slaves out of them.

I pedaled home as fast as I could. When I got back, Mrs. Moody was telling Rosebud to be more careful where he slung his paint on account of she didn't need her zinnias painted white.

I gave the milk shakes to Rosebud, and he said I'd won the bet because he could only drink two. I drank one and gave the other to Mr. Crabtree.

As soon as Biggie got home, I told her about the biker asking about her in Mr. Peoples's place.

"Are you sure he said *my* name?" she asked.

"Yes'm. Mrs. Fiona Wooten Weatherford. That's what he said." Then I told her about the tattoo.

"Well," Biggie said, "if that young man wants to find me, he'll be able to do it. Right now, I could eat a horse and wagon. Wonder if Willie Mae's got supper ready."

Willie Mae did. She'd made fried chicken with red pepper sprinkled on it and fried okra and mashed potatoes, my favorite meal except when she gets too much red pepper on there and it burns my tongue. Willie Mae says if I think that's hot, I oughta taste her *grand-mère's boudin.*

"What's that, Willie Mae?" I asked.

"Blood sausage," she said and turned to talk to Biggie. "Miss Biggie, do you reckon somebody poisoned the mayor like that Chief Trotter say?"

"We may never know now," Biggie answered. "Irwin Smitt's assistant, Larry Jack, who just got out of undertaking school, got so excited about having the mayor for his first customer that he embalmed him right away before they had a chance to tell him they were sending him to Tyler for an autopsy. What's for dessert?"

"Rice pudding with caramel sauce," Willie Mae said, and she went out to the kitchen to serve it up.

While we were having dessert, Biggie remembered something. "J.R. honey, run bring me my black purse, the one I carried to the meeting last night."

When I brought it to her, she reached inside and dug out that old dirty towel she'd stolen from Mr. Popolus's café. She smelled it then shook it out over the table. A little white pill rolled out. Biggie picked it up and held it to the light.

"Can't tell a thing about it." She handed it to Willie Mae. "Does this look familiar to you, Willie Mae?"

Willie Mae held the pill as far from her eyes as she could reach and stared hard at it.

While she was thinking, Biggie said, "Willie Mae, if you'll go to the eye doctor, I'll pay for your glasses."

"My eyes are as good as the day I was born," Willie Mae said and handed the pill back to Biggie. "Could be most anything. The writing's all wore off it."

"Well, don't you have any ideas?"

"No'm. I mostly deal in powders and potions—not pills. Why don't you take it down to Mr. Plumley at the drugstore? He can prob'ly tell you."

"I'll do that tomorrow. Meantime, J.R., get me a little bitty piece of aluminum foil to wrap this in. And put this towel in a plastic bag and put it in the freezer."

Just as I was closing the freezer, the back door slammed and Rosebud walked in, went to the stove, and poured himself a cup of coffee.

"That you, Rosebud?" Biggie called from the dining room. "Come in here. I want to talk to you."

"Yes'm, but I aim to finish that fence tomorrow. That there Miz Moody, she'll talk your ear into a bow knot. I couldn't get nothin' done today for her jabberin' away at me."

"That's not what I want to talk to you about, Rosebud. Sit down and tell me what y'all found in the alley."

"Well, the rain washed away whatever footprints might of been left. Onliest thing else down there was that there town dog's belongings."

"I brought some clues, Biggie. Remember?" I said.

"Sure you did, honey. Bring me that sack out of my dresser drawer."

Biggie shoved her plate out of the way and dumped the stuff I'd found out on the table. She picked up the Grapette bottle cap.

"Hmm—interesting. They haven't made those in years. That cap must be thirty years old. Was it just lying on top of the ground?"

"Yes'm."

Then she started pawing through the broken glass I'd collected. She held one dark blue piece up to the light.

"This looks like it came from an old jar of Vicks salve. Remember that, Willie Mae?"

"Sure do. Many's the days my kids was sent off to school with a granny rag soaked in Vicks salve."

Biggie picked up a scrap of clear glass. "Looky here," she said. "This one is a perfect rectangle—and curved. Wonder what it came from. And look at this, brown. Must have come from a snuff bottle."

She swept all the glass back into the sack, then pulled out the hatband I'd found. "What's this?"

"That's mine," I said. "I'm going to make Booger a collar out of it."

Biggie was staring at the hatband like she'd never seen an old piece of leather before in her life. "I think we'll just keep this for a while, J.R. In a case of murder, you never can tell what's important." She stood up and stretched. "Think I'll go sit on the front porch and rock and think until bedtime."

I decided to catch a few lightning bugs even though I'm too grown up for that. I found an empty mayonnaise jar and waited until they started blinking their lights under the big pecan tree, then I went after them. I pretended they were aliens from the planet Zircon come to examine us earthlings by entering our brains through our ears. I saw one going up under the mock orange tree and dove in after him. Mock oranges have long thorns, so I had to be real careful. When I got up under there, the Zirconian got away, but I found some papers stuck on the thorny branches. I pulled them off and was going into the house to throw them away when Biggie stopped me.

"What's that, honey?" she asked from the porch.

"Just some old papers," I said. "Musta come out of Mr. Crabtree's car."

"Let me see them. Turn on the porch light. Hmm. What do you know? What do you know about that?"

"About what, Biggie?"

"About the fact that these are blank lease forms—coal-lease forms. Looks like our Mr. Crabtree's not all he claims to be."

"Are you going to say anything to him?"

"Not on your life, honey—and you're not either. We've got

to get this murder solved. Then we'll deal with Mr. Wade Hampton Crabtree." Biggie yawned a big old yawn. "Let's go to bed now. Don't you dare tell anybody about this, you hear?"

10

When I came down for breakfast the next morning, Mr. Crabtree was standing on the coffee table wearing Great-Grandpa Wooten's World War I uniform.

"The trousers are a little too long," Biggie said, "but with the puttees nobody will be able to tell."

"Miss Biggie, there's still time for me to send to Mississippi for my own grandfather's Confederate uniform. I really think—"

"Don't be silly, honey. Who ever heard of a Confederate uniform being worn with a coonskin cap?"

Mr. Crabtree opened his mouth to answer, then shut it.

"J.R., don't you think Mr. Crabtree looks dashing?"

"No'm. Can I have waffles for breakfast?"

Biggie was already busy pinning medals on Mr. Crabtree and didn't hear me, so I went into the kitchen to talk to Willie Mae. She was taking a pan of homemade cinnamon rolls out of the oven. I forgot all about waffles.

"Get you some milk out of the fridge and come set down,"

she said. "Your Biggie wants you to go downtown with her directly she gets done with Stonewall Jackson out there."

"Willie Mae, don't you like Mr. Crabtree?"

"It ain't a question of like. He's crooked as the devil's backbone."

"How do you know?"

"I was born with the veil over my eyes. I see things."

"What things?"

"None of your business—and don't talk with your mouth full."

I was just finishing the last of my cinnamon roll when we heard a crash in the living room. We both rushed in there and saw Mr. Crabtree on the floor flapping around like a chicken with its neck wrung.

"Ow! My ankle," he said. "The pain! The pain!"

Biggie said, "Willie Mae, help me get him in a chair so I can see how badly he's hurt."

"It's broken! I'm injured. Oh, Miss Biggie, it looks like I'll be unable to march in the parade after all."

Biggie took off his shoe and felt his ankle. "No, honey, it's not broken," she said. "Still, you might have a bad sprain. Willie Mae, you go get an ice pack. We'll just put Mr. Crabtree up in the guest room until he's better." She patted him on the arm. "You can bet the baby's milk money you won't be able to go upstairs to your apartment for a day or two."

"Miss Biggie, it has been my heart's desire to assist you by representing your noble family in the Pioneer Days festivities, but in my hapless state, I fear I will be of little use to you."

"Never mind, honey. J.R., you go up to the garage apartment and bring down Mr. Crabtree's pajamas and toothbrush while Willie Mae and I assist him to the guest room."

"Wait!" Mr. Crabtree looked plumb panic struck.

"What's the matter, honey?" Biggie asked.

"Well, er—I don't need anything now. Why not wait until evening? I may be better by then."

"Nonsense. Go on, J.R. Hurry, we've got to go downtown."

"No!" Mr. Crabtree stood up and hobbled to the door. "Look, it's better already. I'll just toddle on home now."

He bowed to Biggie and disappeared out the back door.

"Well, I'll be switched," Biggie said.

I looked out the window just in time to see him taking the steps up the side of the garage two at a time.

"Looks to me like he don't want nobody messin' around his place," Willie Mae said.

"Wonder what he's got to hide," Biggie said. "I just wonder—well, never mind. Let's go, J.R., we've got more important business downtown."

Plumley's Drug Emporium is the oldest drugstore in the Ark-La-Tex. It's an old-timey brick building on the corner of Main and Tyler. Eighteen seventy-seven is cut in the stone out front because that was when it was built. Mr. Plumley has it painted bright red with white trim. It has a real soda fountain, which is pink and green with pink and green plastic stools and pink marble on the counter. In back, where they keep the milk-shake machines and glasses and stuff, are some big pictures of sodas and sundaes and banana splits which Mr. Plumley says are valuable on account of the fact that Roderick Cooper, who painted them when he was a teenager, went off to Hollywood and became a famous set designer. Miss Jewelene MacLeod works there and is very old and has to wear a green uniform with pink trim on the collar and sleeves and a pink handkerchief in her pocket. She says that color doesn't do a thing for her complexion, but I doubt if any color would.

"Hidy, Biggie. Hidy, J.R.," she said when we came in.

" 'Mornin', Jewelene," Biggie said. "Dedrick in?"

"He's back in the back mixin' up some cough syrup for Itha's boy. Why don't y'all have something to drink while you wait?"

Biggie had coffee and I just had a cherry Coke because I was still full of Willie Mae's cinnamon rolls. In a few minutes, Mr. Plumley came out from behind the big wall where he mixes up prescriptions.

" 'Mornin', Biggie. What can I do for you?"

Biggie pulled out the little pill she'd dug out of the mayor's mouth and, being real careful, took it out of the aluminum foil it was wrapped in.

"What would you say this is, Dedrick?"

"Hmm," Mr. Plumley said. "Can't say as I know. Could be most anything from Lasix to digitalis. The identification's pert' near rubbed off. Where'd you get it?"

"Out of Mayor Gribbons's mouth the night he died," Biggie said.

"Oh. That might explain it, then. The mayor took nitroglycerin for his heart, and it's a little white pill just like this one. I just refilled his prescription last Monday."

"Yes, but are you sure that's what *this* pill is?" Biggie asked. "Dedrick, I'd be much obliged if you'd just go back there and double-check—and, while you're at it, would you just see what else he was taking?"

When he came back, Mr. Plumley looked like he'd just dropped his chewing gum in a chicken yard. "Well, I'll be switched," he said. "This here's ephedrine—a bronchodilator. He ought not to of been takin' that."

Biggie had perked up right smart. "Why do you say that?" she asked.

"On account of his heart, don'cha know. What with his heart and his high blood pressure, this stuff could of been downright bad for him. Wait a minute! I need to check something else."

Mr. Plumley went back to the pharmacy and came back shaking his head.

"Just what I thought," he said. "Old Doc Hooper had him on thyroid medicine on account of him being so fat. Oh, lordy, Biggie, he ought not to of been taking ephedrine."

"Where do you reckon he got it?" Biggie asked.

"It's over-the-counter. Lots of folks take it for energy—or to lose weight. I don't sell it. They'd have to go over to Center Point to get it."

He shoved the little pill back toward Biggie and she wrapped it up and put it back in her purse.

When we got back home, Willie Mae was making fried cornbread. Rosebud was sitting at the table watching her and drinking a glass of buttermilk. Booger had jumped up on the counter and was washing his hind foot. Biggie picked up Booger and tossed him out the back door then came and sat down by Rosebud. She told them what Mr. Plumley had said about the mayor's pills.

"Who 'round here you reckon would be takin' that there ephi—that stuff what the drugstore man said it was?" Rosebud asked. "Seems to me like that's what we got to find out."

"I agree," Biggie said, "but Mr. Plumley says you can buy it over the counter. It could be most anybody."

"Didn't you say they takes it for energy?"

"That's right, Rosebud! Let's think about who has more energy than they've a right to have."

"Mr. Thripp," I said. "He's always out mowing his yard and working in the flower beds. He's thin, too!"

"And Butch," said Willie Mae. "That boy hops around like a little flea. Couldn't nobody keep up with him."

"Then there's Jimmie Sue," said Biggie. "She reminds me of a cheerleader the way she's always on the go."

"What about that there Mr. Crabtree," Willie Mae said.

"Seems like he's gone from daylight to dark sellin' them funeral policies of his."

"That's right," Biggie said, standing up, "and there's no time like the present. He's already under suspicion on account of those coal-lease forms J.R. found. Maybe it's time we had a peek into his quarters. Is he home now?"

"No'm. He left soon after y'all did—walkin' good as ever. What makes you think the mayor didn't buy that stuff hisself?"

"Because, since he got so fat he never left Kemp County. Used to pride himself on it—said everything he needed was right here in Job's Crossing." She got the key to the garage apartment off the nail on the back porch. "Now, let's go see what Mr. Wade Hampton Crabtree's got to hide."

Me and Rosebud followed her up the outside stairs to the apartment.

I was nervous as a kitten up a tree but Biggie said not to worry, Willie Mae was going to blow Great-Grandpa Wooten's bugle if she saw Mr. Crabtree coming back.

The place was clean as a brand-new pair of tennis shoes. You couldn't even find a hair in his comb, which was lined up in a row on the dresser with his two silver brushes and his old-timey straight razor.

Biggie said, "Rosebud, you take the closet; I'll take the dresser drawers. J.R., you check the bathroom."

I didn't find a thing in the bathroom but a velour robe and a pair of black leather bedroom slippers. The bath mat was hung, straight as a guitar string, on the tub, and the soap looked brand-new.

Biggie was digging in the dresser drawers and mumbling about how she didn't trust anyone this neat.

Rosebud was on his hands and knees looking on the closet floor. "Dog my cats," he said. "What do you know 'bout that." He came out holding a pair of shiny black cowboy boots. "You ever see him wear anything like this?"

"Gracious, no," Biggie said. "He dresses more like Colonel Sanders than Roy Rogers. Why would he have those?"

By now Rosebud was going through his clothes. "Hot dog!" he said. "Looky here!"

He pulled out a pair of ironed jeans, a red cowboy shirt, and a black leather vest.

"Look for a hat," Biggie said.

Rosebud pulled a hat box down from the shelf and opened it on the bed. He pulled out Mr. Crabtree's Panama that he had been wearing when the car blew up. Underneath, he found a black, flat-brim felt hat.

"Hmm," Biggie said. "Rosebud, do you think this would go with western gear?"

"Well'm, seems like I recollect seein' Wyatt Earp wear a hat like this on a TV show. Onliest thing is, he had a band on it—with conchos all around. This here hat ain't got no band."

"So it doesn't," Biggie said. "J.R., right after lunch, you and I are taking a little drive out to the farm. I need to talk to Coye about that little sidewinder wanting to lease my land."

"You think it was Mr. Crabtree, Biggie?"

"I'd bet the farm on it, honey. Now, scoot! Willie Mae's got lunch ready."

Biggie decided to lie down and take a nap before going to the farm so I got on my bike and rode downtown. As I passed city hall, I saw a big black wreath on the door. In gold letters across the front, it said OSBERT GRIBBONS, R.I.P. Butch was sitting on the iron bench in front of his flower shop. I sat down beside him.

When Butch first came to town fifteen years ago wearing his hair long and dressing in ladies' clothes, old Judge Pitts, who was judge before Judge Grimes took over, wanted to throw him in jail for being a public nuisance and disturbing the peace, but Biggie told him to leave Butch alone or she'd tell everybody about the time back in 'forty-seven when he, Judge Pitts, had got kicked out of the Shriners for letting a whore wear his fez right there in the lobby of the Baker Hotel in Dallas when they were having their convention.

"Did you make that wreath for Mayor Gribbons?" I asked.

"Oh, yes," Butch said. "I designed it myself. The ribbon is genuine rayon sateen—all the way from Saint Louis. Don't you just love it?"

"I guess so. Hey, how come you got that nail polish on your toenails?" I said, looking down at his sandals. "I've never seen a man—"

"What's the matter?" Butch asked, holding his feet out in front of him. "Don't you like this color?" he asked. "It's called Passionfire. I've got another color called Tropical Orchid but it doesn't match this shirt I'm wearing."

I decided to change the subject. "Did your mime costume come in yet?"

"Oh, J.R. I wish you hadn't mentioned it," Butch said. "I'm just as distraught as can be. The costume company in New Orleans sent me a fax. They're all out of mime costumes. I asked if they had any harlequin suits, but they were out of those, too." He clasped his hands together between his knees. "I don't know what I'm going to do. I had my heart set on being a mime this year."

"Why can't you just be old-timey like everybody else?" I asked. "Biggie could probably find you something to wear."

"I guess I'll have to," Butch said. "But I had my heart set on that mime costume—had the cutest act worked out. I would of knocked 'em dead, J.R."

"I bet I know who can help you," I said. "Willie Mae. You know—Willie Mae that works for Biggie!"

Butch looked at me like I'd lost my mind.

"Come on," I said. "You don't know Willie Mae. She's magic. Come on!"

Butch locked the door to the flower shop and we walked back to Biggie's house with me pushing my bike. I led Butch around back and tapped on Willie Mae's door.

"Whatchall want?" she said, opening the door just a crack.

When I told her about Butch's costume, she let us in and started in rummaging around in her old cedar chest, mumbling to herself.

"Are you saying voodoo spells, Willie Mae?" I asked.

"No, I ain't saying no spells. I'm asking myself questions," she said. "Now you just go on back in the house. I hear your Biggie callin'. Mor'n likely she's ready to go to the farm. Go on, now!"

"Are you gonna help Butch?"

"What does it look like I'm doing. Now git!"

As I left, I saw she had a big pile of bright-colored cloth on the floor beside the cedar chest. Butch looked happier than a pig in sunshine.

11

Miss Biggie, when they gonna funeralize the mayor?" Willie Mae asked after lunch.

"Tomorrow. They had to wait for his brother to come from Phoenix." Biggie slapped her forehead. "My gracious, I almost forgot. Willie Mae, would you please press J.R.'s suit? He'll have to wear it to the services."

"Aw, Biggie," I said. "I don't have to go, do I?"

She said I had to go on account of I was her right-hand man, and she needed my eyes and ears.

"Now, go get my opera glasses out of the hall closet. I'm going to inspect that dratted dump while we're at the farm."

On the drive out, I said, "Biggie, do you remember the other night when we had the meeting and right after that the mayor was killed?"

"Of course I remember, J.R.," she said. "We were just talking about it. What's the matter with you?"

"Well, you remember I was back in the shelves looking at the old court records?"

"Um-hum."

"Well, Biggie, I found something funny there. It was about James Royce Wooten."

"Um-hum. Look, J.R., the sweet-gum trees are starting to turn. Before you know it, it'll be fall."

"Biggie, this is important. Listen—I found an old law in one of those books. It said even though James Royce left a family back in Tennessee, it was hereby decreed, declared, and directed that his heirs and assigns here in Texas were hereinafter deemed legitimate and could inherit from his estate under the law. What do you think that means, Biggie?"

"I declare, honey, you talk just like your grandpa, Eldridge Wooten. You'll make a lawyer when you grow up. That's for sure."

"But, Biggie, what does all that mean?"

"It means that James Royce had a family back in Tennessee that he probably meant to send for when he got settled here in Texas but never quite got around to. Happened all the time with those early settlers. This was the frontier, remember. They made up new rules as they went along."

"Does that mean I've got cousins in Tennessee I don't even know?"

"Probably, honey."

"Did you know about it, Biggie?"

"Um-hum."

All of a sudden I remembered seeing the biker at Mr. Peoples's place. "Biggie, that biker had a tattoo on his arm just like your family crest. Reckon he's one of those cousins?"

"I'm going to have to think on that, honey," Biggie said. "Look, there's Monica. You run on and play while I talk to Coye and Ernestine."

"Hey, Miss Biggie. Hey, J.R.," Mrs. Sontag said. "Y'all want a piece of coconut pie? I just this minute cut a piece for Coye."

"Ernestine, your pie would make a bulldog break his chain. I sure would enjoy a piece. How about you, J.R.?"

"Yes'm. I'd rather eat pie than play."

The Sontags' kitchen is a long room on the back of the house with a big window that looks out over the fields and trees. Over to the right, you can see the stock pond where Monica and me like to catch crawdads. The table is round and covered with a tablecloth that has red geraniums on it, and Mrs. Sontag keeps a big wooden bowl full of fruit in the middle. The kitchen always smells like something good is cooking: mayhaw jelly boiling or chicken frying. What I like best is when Mrs. Sontag bakes cakes and pies. It's a mystery to me how Mr. Sontag stays so skinny.

Mrs. Sontag brought out the pie and we all sat in cane-bottom chairs around the table.

"Coye," Biggie said, "I want you to tell me everything you can remember about that feller that was wanting to lease this property."

Mr. Sontag stretched out his legs and squinted his eyes and thought real hard. I think it was an effort. Then he said, "Well'm, he was all duded out like one of them picture-show cowboys, don'cha know. Lash LaRue or some of them."

"That's right," Mrs. Sontag said. "Don't nobody around here dress like that, do they, Papa?"

"Yeah," Monica said. "Once I saw a cowboy in a movie dressed like that, but it was in California or Mexico, or some-where—not Texas."

"I'll tell you who he reminded me of," said Mrs. Sontag. "He reminded me of the Cisco Kid—remember him?"

Biggie nodded. "Exactly what was he wearing?"

Mr. Sontag scratched his head. "Don't reckon I recollect what the feller was wearing. You, Mama?"

"Not so's you could tell it. Flashy, sort of."

"I remember," Monica said. "He had on a black leather

vest and a hat with conchos on the band. And a red shirt. Yeah, red with pearl buttons."

Biggie stood up. "Well, thanks for the pie, Ernestine. J.R. and I have to go now. We're planning to inspect the dump before we go back to town."

"Biggie," I said, "can Monica spend the night at our house before the parade?"

"Sure, honey. You plan on that now, Monica. You hear?"

Monica grinned a big old grin. "Sure!"

Biggie drove the car over to the Wooten family graveyard and parked under a big oak tree.

"Hand me my opera glasses, J.R.," she said. "Well, bless Pat, looks like they've got the dang blasted thing finished. There's trash in there already."

"Let me look, Biggie."

Sure enough, the bottom was covered with trash bags and cartons and I even saw an old rocking chair someone had thrown out. I looked up at the sky and saw buzzards circling overhead.

Biggie took the binoculars back and looked for a long time. Finally, she said, "Come on, J.R. We've got um now."

She got out of the car and started scrambling down the hill. "Bring that plastic bag out of the backseat," she hollered over her shoulder. She ran to the edge of the pit and looked down.

"What, Biggie?" I panted. "What do you see down there?"

She shaded her eyes with her hand and pointed. "See that dead dog?"

"Yes'm."

"Well, honey, I want you to take this sack and go get me that dog. Bring him right back. You hear? Yessiree! We've got um now."

I knew that dog. It was Ralph, the town dog. He wasn't nothing but a little terrier, so he wasn't heavy. But if you've never tried to stuff a dead dog that's already gone stiff in a plastic bag, well, I'll be the first to tell you, it ain't easy. I finally got all four legs in and scrunched up the top of the bag.

"Biggie, what you gonna do with him, anyway? Are you gonna get Willie Mae to do a hex with him?"

"No, honey, this dead dog is evidence, pure and simple. They've got no right to go dumping dead animals in the dump. They've got to be buried. It's the law."

When we got home, Biggie said, "Now, put that dog in the freezer, J.R.—and don't be doing your face like that. We've got to keep him nice and fresh."

I went outside and sat on the back steps to think about that. I watched Booger sitting on the fence while Mrs. Moody's little dog about had a conniption fit trying to get to him. Bumblebees were dive-bombing the honeysuckle. Pretty soon Rosebud came out and sat beside me.

"Hush your mouth, dog," he hollered at Prissy. "You be sorry if you ever catch that cat, let me tell you." He took out a can of Copenhagen and put a pinch of snuff in his mouth. "What's troublin' you, cher? Seems to me like you carryin' around a load of worrisomeness."

"Rosebud," I said, "did you ever hear 'bout anybody that kept dead dogs in the freezer?"

"Nope."

"What about catfish in the toilet?"

He scratched his head while he thought about that. "Can't say I has," he said.

"Well then, did you ever in your life hear of anybody washing their greens in the bathtub—or putting their feet in the fridge?"

"No sirree bob. Not none of that."

"Well, Rosebud, why do you reckon Biggie does those things?"

Rosebud put his arm across my shoulders. "Why don't

you ask me something hard?" he asked. "Your Biggie does all those things because she's of a creative turn of mind—and she ain't got time to worry about the stuff most folks worry about. You ever hear of Benjamin Franklin?"

"Sure."

"Well, what d'ya think all them folks back then thought when he commenced flyin' a kite right in the middle of a gully washer?"

"I guess they might of thought he was crazy."

"Okay, let me ask you another one. What d'ya reckon they thought when old Hannibal took a notion to cross the Alps with a bunch of elephants?"

"Crazy?"

"I 'spect so. And what about old Justin Hebert, who went shrimpin' usin' a army-surplus parachute for a net?"

"Crazy? What happened to him? Did he bring home the biggest load of shrimp ever?"

"Hell, no, boy. That there parachute filled up with water and capsized his boat ass over teakettle. Old Hebert would of drowned if me and Boudreaux hadn't been shrimpin' in the area. We pulled him out and took him home. Mrs. Hebert wouldn't speak to him for five months runnin'. Feel better now, cher?"

"I don't know; I guess so. One thing's for sure, Biggie ain't likely to change, and I don't guess I'd want her to."

Just then, Willie Mae's head popped around the screen door. "Y'all git on in here now," she said. "Supper's on the table."

The next day was Mayor Gribbons's funeral. Biggie made me put on my Sunday school suit and a white shirt. She made Rosebud put on a suit to drive us to the church.

"You look real nice," she said. "Now, go comb your hair—and put water on it so it'll stay down in back."

Biggie wore her navy blue dress with the big white polka dots. "Oh, this is too drab," she said. "Willie Mae, hand me those silk roses out of the drawer."

"Them things is all mashed up," Willie Mae said. "You don't want to wear them, Miss Biggie."

"Well, what about a scarf then."

"Onliest one you got is brown with yellow giraffes on it. Wait a minute. I'll be right back."

Willie Mae went out the door and came back in a few minutes carrying her silk scarf Sister Sylvester had given her.

"This'll brighten you up inside *and* out," she said.

"Perfect!" Biggie said. "Let's go, J.R. We don't want to miss the viewing."

When we got to the Baptist church, they had the casket right at the entry—open so you had to look in. I gotta admit, old Larry Jack did a good job on the mayor. His face wasn't black anymore, like it was when Biggie pulled it up out of his cake, and his cheeks were real rosy. Larry Jack even put a big smile on his face, like he was just getting ready to kiss a baby or something.

Mr. and Mrs. Muckleroy and Miss Mattie were standing by the casket.

"I swan," said Miss Mattie, "if he don't look better'n life. That Larry Jack's an artist—a pure-dee artist!"

"And would you look at all the flowers," said Mrs. Muckleroy. "I don't believe I've ever seen this church so full of flowers."

"Well, honey, "Biggie said, "he can't enjoy them now, and where he is, I doubt he ever will."

About that time, Norman Thripp came walking up the sidewalk. "It's a sad thing," he said, "a sad, sad, thing. As your acting mayor pro tem, I have declared today Osbert Gribbons Day."

I guess everybody in town was in church that day, and

Brother Parker wasn't about to pass up an opportunity like that. He must of preached a good forty-five minutes, then passed the collection plate. After that, Mr. Thripp gave the eulogy and we sang "Nothing but the Blood of Jesus." Then we all got in our cars and had a funeral procession out to the town cemetery. Chief Trotter and Jimmie Sue led in the police car with the lights on.

At the cemetery, they had put up a big green tent and, somehow, the funeral-home people had managed to get all the flowers out of the church and piled around the grave. Butch was there wearing his crushed-velvet suit with a white poet's blouse. He kept moving the flowers around so they'd show up better. You couldn't even tell there was a hole in the ground on account of they'd put down a big green cloth, and the coffin was hanging over it. Brother Parker started in talking again, and pretty soon he had the whole crowd sniffing and crying even though most of them didn't care much for the mayor when he was alive. I was waiting for Brother Parker to pass the collection plate again when Biggie let out a holler and fell to the ground.

I screamed, "Biggie!" and dropped down beside her. Just before the others gathered around, she looked up at me and winked.

"It's Biggie!" someone yelled. "Get the doctor. Quick!"

"Dr. Hooper!" hollered Chief Trotter. "Get over here. Hurry!"

Then things really got confused; everyone was talking at once. Mrs. Muckleroy was sure Biggie'd had a stroke on account of she said all the Wootens are prone to high blood pressure. Miss Mattie was of the opinion that Biggie was overcome with emotion after that fine sermon Brother Parker preached, but Mr. Thripp said Biggie Weatherford had never been overcome by emotion about anything, least of all one of Brother Parker's sermons. Jimmie Sue thought it must of been something she ate.

I stood aside next to Rosebud and watched while they loaded Biggie into the hearse and raced away to the hospital. All the funeral cars followed behind, leaving the mayor hanging over his grave in the middle of all his flowers.

12

The Kemp County Memorial Hospital is located right smack-dab in the middle between Job's Crossing and Center Point on Farm to Market Road 57. They built it there because the citizens of the two towns couldn't agree on where to put it. The Center Point folks said it should be in Center Point on account of they had the most doctors; the Job's Crossing folks insisted it should be in Job's Crossing on account of all they had was Doc Hooper, and most of them would probably die if they didn't have at least a fighting chance of getting to a decent doctor.

Me and Rosebud followed the ambulance in Biggie's car until we got to the Pixley crossing. Rosebud said he knew a shortcut to get there but he made a wrong turn and landed us at Hope Chapel, which is way the other side of Center Point. By the time we got to the hospital, Biggie was already sitting up in bed wearing a pink-and-white-striped hospital gown. She started right in giving orders.

She told Rosebud to go home and get her pink flow-eredy gown and her face powder and her toothbrush and that sticky stuff she uses to hold her upper plate in.

"Can I stay here with you, Biggie?" I asked.

"Sure, honey," she said. "I need to talk to you anyway."

After Rosebud left, she said, "J.R., honey, Biggie's not really sick. She's just got to make some folks think so for a while. Will you promise not to tell a soul?"

I promised, but didn't tell her I already knew she wasn't sick. I've seen Biggie when she's sick, and it ain't a pretty sight. She gets all gray and grumpy. Today she was beaming like a game-show host.

The door opened, and Dr. Hooper came shuffling in. "Wellsirree, how's our prettiest patient feeling now she's all snug in bed?"

"Honey, I feel about as pretty as you think I am," Biggie said, not smiling. "It's my heart, Doctor. I know it. I'm going to just fade away like my Grandmother Fletcher—one day she was digging a well and the next, poof, she was dead as a hammer. Her heart took her, just like that."

Biggie's face took on a grayish color and she seemed to sink down into her pillow and get smaller as she talked.

Dr. Hooper took out his stethoscope and started listening to her chest. "Ummm," he said. Then he made her sit up while he listened from the back a while.

"Biggie, I'm afraid you're right," he said. "We may be dealing with a diseased heart here. Shall I send you to Tyler for another opinion?"

"Oh, no, honey," Biggie said, almost purring. "I've got all the confidence in the world in you. Why, you've treated everybody in town for years and years. If anybody knows hearts, it's you."

I couldn't believe what I was hearing. I'd heard Biggie say

a thousand times she wouldn't trust Dr. Hooper to peddle a pill to a polecat.

"Biggie!" I said after he'd gone.

"It's okay, honey," she said. "I've got a mind to take me a good rest, and I aim to do it right here in the Kemp County Memorial Hospital."

When Rosebud came back with Biggie's things, I went home with him for the night. The next morning Willie Mae, Rosebud, and I came back to the hospital just as Biggie was polishing off a big breakfast of scrambled eggs and sausage and hot cakes with butter and syrup.

"Um-um, that was good," she said. "Lucky for me Dr. Hooper never even *heard* of cholesterol." She handed the tray to Willie Mae. "Put this on the table, honey. We've got to get down to work."

"What kind of work, Biggie?" I asked.

"Figuring out what's going on in Job's Crossing and putting a stop to it," Biggie said. "First the city decides to build a dump right next to the Wooten family graveyard, which is bad enough in itself, but then some out-of-state bozos take a sudden notion that Kemp County is a good place to punch holes and scrape up the countryside looking for lignite."

I was getting the idea. "That's right, Biggie. Then Mr. Crabtree's car gets exploded."

"On top of that, the mayor goes and gets hisself deader'n a armadillo crossin' a freeway," Rosebud said.

"Exactly," Biggie said.

"And his pills wasn't what they was supposed to be," Willie Mae said. "What you gonna do, Miss Biggie?"

"Get to the bottom of it," Biggie said. "Something tells me these events are all connected somehow. Now, where do we start?"

"I say start with that there Crabtree," Rosebud said. "I

once known a feller like him. He'd lie when the truth would do just as good."

"That's right, honey," Biggie said, "and from the evidence we have right now, it looks pretty obvious that he was the peckerwood going around the county trying to buy up coal leases."

"How come you say that, Miss Biggie?" Willie Mae asked.

"Well, for starters, J.R. found blank lease forms under a bush in my front yard. We figured they must have come from his car when it exploded—although that may not be true. They *could* have come from somewhere else."

"So, Miss Biggie, what else you got on him?"

"I know, Biggie," I said. "The clothes. Monica and her mama and daddy described the clothes we found in Mr. Crabtree's closet exactly—all except for the concho hatband. They were the clothes the lease man was wearing."

"And we've found the conchos and the hatband," Biggie said.

"That's right, Biggie. Behind the café the day after Mayor Gribbons died. I'll bet he put something in the mayor's cake."

"That's all very well," Biggie said, "but why would he want the mayor dead? Besides, that dog might have found that hatband somewhere else and drug it there. Didn't you say he had a shoe and some bones there, too?"

"That's right," I said. "I used to see Ralph all the time carrying stuff back there."

"And I don't see a way in the world to connect Wade Crabtree with those pills the mayor was taking. If someone actually switched his pills, it would have to have been someone close to him, someone who could watch and wait for an opportunity."

"He didn't have no family, did he, Miss Biggie?" Rosebud asked.

"Only his brother. And he was in Phoenix."

Willie Mae spoke up. "I think there's one thing y'all's for-gettin'. Somebody blowed up old Crabtree's car for him. You reckon he done that to himself?"

"No, I don't, Willie Mae," Biggie said. "There's more to this than just Crabtree coming here and pretending to be something he wasn't just to take coal leases."

"So what are you gonna do, Biggie?" I asked.

"I'm going to lie right here in this bed and let that old quack Hooper pretend he's treating me for a bad heart. Before long the whole town will be coming out here to find out if I'm dying. It's the perfect opportunity to question each and every one of them." She patted my hand. "J.R., why don't you get some change out of my purse and go down to the snack bar and get us all a cold drink. I'm dry as one of Brother Parker's sermons."

I took the money and went down on the elevator to the first floor. As I passed the reception desk, I heard somebody call my name.

"Why J.R. Weatherford. Howth your grandmothah? Can she have vithitorth yet?"

It was Miss Lonie Fulkerson, and she was wearing a pink coat with VOLUNTEER written on the pocket.

"Yes'm, I guess so."

"Ith she feeling better? Doth she have to have oxygen? Doth she have an IV in her arm?"

"No'm. I gotta go."

"You tell her I'll be up to thee her juth as thoon ath I get off. You hear?"

"Yes'm."

The snack bar is way at the other end of the hospital. I had to pass the O.B. ward to get there, so I stopped and watched the babies for a while. Those babies couldn't do anything except scream their heads off or suck on their pacifiers. A whole family, grandparents and a new mama and daddy, were standing there just grinning their heads off at one of the babies. Personally, I'd rather have an iguana.

Farther down, I found the snack bar, a little room at the end of the hall where they have vending machines and four tables with chairs. Three nurses were sitting in one corner drinking coffee. I heard one say, "Keeled over right there at the funeral. They say it's her heart."

A big fat nurse with the blackest hair I ever saw said, "If she dies, someone's gonna be mighty rich. That old woman owns half the county."

Then one said, "Shh!" and they got real quiet.

I got me and Rosebud strawberries and Biggie and Willie Mae colas, and hurried out of there. They could think what they wanted. I knew Biggie wasn't going to die. Or was she? Maybe Biggie wasn't telling me the truth. Maybe she really was sick. All of a sudden I felt like I'd just swallowed a rock. But Biggie always told the truth—to me, at least. I took the drinks and hurried out of there.

I didn't stop to watch the babies on the way back. I wanted to see Biggie again, just to remind myself that she was healthy as always and just pretending to be sick to solve a mystery. I was telling myself that and not looking where I was going when I ran smack into someone and felt two hands grab me by the shoulders. I held on to the drinks, but as I was trying to get my balance back, I looked down and saw two black boots, with square toes. I made myself look up, and on the way from the feet to the face I saw big hands with leather wristbands and a familiar tattoo. The biker. I wriggled free and ran as fast as I could down the hall. I could hear his feet running after me.

I thought I heard him call out to me, "Wait! Stop!" but you can bet your last marble I wasn't about to. I was trying to decide whether to go to the elevator and take a chance of him catching me or take the stairs that are deserted most of the time so that, if he did catch me, he could kill me and leave my bloody body there and they might not find me for no telling how long, when I came to a big green door and ducked inside. I heard his feet clomping down the hall just as the door closed. I stood there panting and looked around. The room was painted an ugly green and had a stainless-steel sink at one side. Along one wall, I could see what looked like huge drawers, all closed. Then I saw it. A gurney was parked along one wall and there was something on it—something covered with a sheet, but not quite. A hand was hanging from under the sheet. I got out of there fast, just hoping and praying that I could make it back to Biggie's room before the biker found me. I ran to the lobby and, thank goodness, the elevator doors were open. I hopped aboard and as soon as it stopped on Biggie's floor, I flew back to her room and fell across her bed, panting.

"Honey, what's wrong?" Biggie said. "You look like you've got a rattlesnake in your sleeping bag."

All of a sudden I felt better. Biggie has that effect on me.

"Oh, nothin'," I said. "I just saw that biker downstairs is all. I'm not afraid of him."

"Sure," Willie Mae said, "that's why you're shakin' like a wet chihuahua."

I was about to argue with her when the door opened and Butch came in carrying the biggest vase of red carnations I'd ever seen. He set them down and perched on the foot of Biggie's bed.

"I had these leftover from the mayor's casket spray, so I just made you a nice arrangement. Don't you think the baby's breath is a nice touch?" He leaned over and kissed Biggie on the cheek. "Biggie, you gave us all such a fright. My heart's still just pounding to beat the band. . . . Sweetie, I just *flew* out here to see about you . . . you know, everybody in town's talking about nothing else!"

Biggie patted his hand. "I know," she said. "The doctor says it's my heart. Honey, you go back to town and tell everybody you see that Biggie Weatherford may not live much longer, and she wants to see all her friends before she passes on."

Butch clasped his hands together and rolled his eyes toward the ceiling. "Ooh, yes. I'll tell them all, Biggie—each and every one! I'll scurry back to town and get started right away. Toodle-oo, everybody!" He hopped off the bed and did a little dance step as he raced out of the room.

"There goes a happy man," Biggie said. "Get those flowers out of here before I suffocate."

13

The next morning, Biggie and I sat in her hospital room and watched television. We were watching a talk show, and this man was telling all about how he'd married his granddaughter's best friend and then cheated on her with his home-health-care nurse. Biggie said it put her in mind of old Leander McNutt from Wells Chapel, only in his case it'd been his great-niece he married and the meter maid over at Center Point he'd been cheating with. Biggie said he wore himself down to nothing but skin and bones trying to keep them happy on account of both being a good bit younger than he was. His doctor told him to give up women and take up another hobby. So he took up whittling and made quite a name for himself as a primitive artist. She said people came from as far away as Waco to buy his whittling over at the bait shop after the lake came in.

She was about to tell me what happened to the meter maid when Elvaree Odum, the nurse, came in and flopped down on a chair. She set the little tray she was carrying on Biggie's bedside table.

"These here are your pills," she said. "Doc says take one now and save the other 'til later in case your heart starts to palpitatin'." She took off her big white nurse's shoes and held her feet up in the air. "I swanny," she said, "my bunions are bigger'n hickory nuts. You ever seen anything like that?"

Biggie leaned over and took a look. "Once," she said. "My cousin, Mozelle Wooten—you remember the twins? Mozelle and Lozelle? Mozelle was the light-complected one. Well, she had these bunions that were so big it looked like she was growing an extra pair of feet on top of the ones she already had." Biggie poured herself a glass of water and took a sip. "She had to order all her shoes out of the catalog, men's size Seven-EEEE. What she did was, she started soaking her feet in alum water every night. Before a year was out, she was wearing a Six-B. Shrunk um down, don'cha know."

Elvaree looked down at her feet. "You reckon that'd help me, Miss Biggie?"

"You try it, honey," Biggie said. "You'll be dancing the Cotton-eyed Joe in no time."

"I will. I sure will!"

Elvaree put on her shoes and left grinning like she'd just won the lottery. She forgot to watch to make sure Biggie took her pill. Biggie dumped one of the pills in the drawer and left the little cup holding the other on her table.

Butch and Miss Lonie must of done a good job passing the word around town about Biggie being in the hospital, because at two the visitors started pouring in. The first was Jimmie Sue wearing a white dress with red buttons. She had a big red bow with white polka dots holding her blond hair back. She looked pretty as a birthday cake.

"How you doin', Miss Biggie?" she asked.

Biggie had turned all gray and shriveled again.

"Not too well, honey," she said. "The doctor says it's my heart."

"Well, looky here what I brought you," Jimmie Sue said. "Guess who's working at the volunteers' desk? Miss Mattie McClure. When she found out I was coming to see you, she made me wait while she went to the cafeteria and had um make up this chocolate milk shake especially for you. J.R., I didn't know you'd be here or I'd of got you one, too."

I said I didn't care because I'd just had a big glass of orange juice, which was true. Biggie set the milk shake on her little table and pulled the hot-water bottle she'd made Elvaree get for her out from under the covers.

"This thing's cold as ice," she said. "Empty it out for me, J.R., and put it right here in my drawer." She smiled at Jimmie Sue. "Now then, you pretty thing, you just sit here and tell me all about what's been going on down at the courthouse."

Jimmie Sue patted Biggie's hand. "Everybody's talking about Norman Thripp," she said. "Miss Biggie, they've got him in jail."

"What on earth for?" Biggie asked.

"Seems the auditors came and found a ten-thousand-dollar shortage in the books. Well, since Mr. Thripp just added a room on his house, they just naturally suspected him. The judge signed a warrant and—"

"My gracious," Biggie said. "Now, what's on your mind? I can see something's bothering you and it's a cinch it's not Norman Thripp stealing from the city."

"You're right," she said. "I don't want to bother you, in your time of sickness, but oh, Miss Biggie, I need to talk to you real bad."

She plucked a tissue out of Biggie's box and started dabbing at her eyes. Biggie perked up and forgot she was supposed to be sick for a minute. Then she went all gray again.

"I'm never too sick to help out a friend in need, honey," she said. "You just tell Biggie what's bothering you."

"It's that biker fellow," Jimmie Sue said. "You heard anything about him?"

"Only a little," Biggie said. "J.R. has seen him several times."

"He was right here in the hospital yesterday," I said. "He tried to grab me, but I got away."

Jimmie Sue started crying. "Oh, Miss Biggie," she said, "I don't know what to do. He's been *stalking* me! Just like that movie I saw on TV. We've got a *stalker* in town, and he's after me!"

"Why, you poor little thing," Biggie said. "Have you told the chief about this?"

"I'm scared to, Miss Biggie. Travis is so jealous. I'm afraid he'll do something that would hurt his career in law enforcement. You know, police brutality or something."

"Well, I can certainly see how you'd feel that way," Biggie said. "Travis Trotter has had a temper ever since he was a boy. I remember the time he got mad at the shop teacher. What was his name, now? I never could remember that boy's name; he was kin to the McMinns over in Prospect—"

Jimmie Sue looked at her wrist. "Miss Biggie," she said, "have you got the time? My watch is in the shop and I've got to—"

"Oh, I remember now," Biggie said. "Frankie Buck Harris, his name was. Anyway, Travis got mad because he said the birdhouse he'd built (Travis, I mean—not Frankie Buck) looked like a chicken coop. He (Travis) poured glue in all the little jars Frankie Buck kept his nuts and bolts in and he (Frankie Buck) had to buy all new ones. You're right. That Travis Trotter's got a mighty hot temper." Biggie looked at her watch. "It's a quarter to three," she said.

111

"But what should I do, Miss Biggie?" Jimmie Sue asked.

"Oh, I'd go ahead and tell Travis," Biggie said. "I doubt if that biker fellow's got any nuts and bolts he don't want glued together."

Just then, the door opened and, before you could skin a skunk, the whole room was full of people. The judge came in carrying a big box of Whitman's chocolates and said Biggie looked radiant as a bride. Biggie told him it wasn't nice to make fun of a poor woman that was on her last legs and could go any minute just like that. Miss Mattie and Miss Lonie came wearing their pink volunteer jackets. Miss Mattie told about the time her uncle's first wife collapsed at a cattle auction and had to be taken to the hospital in a horse trailer.

"She didn't last out the night," she said. "When she got to the undertakers, she still had manure on her heel."

"Biggie, I hope you haven't forgotten how I've alwayth admired your thapphire thtickpin," Miss Lonie said.

"I haven't forgotten, Lonie," Biggie said. "When I go, it's yours."

The door opened again and in walked Butch, carrying the biggest vase of yellow roses I've ever seen.

"Ooh, Biggie," he said, "just look at these darling roses the Daughters sent you—two whole dozen, a dollar and a half each. Where you want me to put them?"

"Put them on my table for now," Biggie said, and slid her hand across the table. When she did, the little cup with the pill fell off on the floor. "My pill," she said, "somebody find my pill! I'm feeling palpitations coming on. Hurry!"

The judge rang for the nurse while the rest of us got down on the floor to look for the pill. Just as Elvaree came hobbling into the room, Jimmie Sue hollered, "I've got it!" and plopped the pill on the table.

Elvaree made everyone leave then and fluffed up Biggie's pillows.

"Thanks, honey," Biggie said. "I'm feeling much better now. I don't believe I'm having palpitations after all."

After supper, Willie Mae and Rosebud came to visit and to take me back home for the night. By that time, Biggie's room looked like Mayor Gribbons's funeral. Butch had been kept busy all day trotting flowers out to the hospital.

Willie Mae got right to the point.

"Miss Biggie, why are you here?" she said. "We know you ain't sick."

"Of course I'm not sick. I'm detecting."

"Miss Biggie," Rosebud said, "have I ever told you about the time I used to be a special investigator for the law firm of Jefferson, Jackson, and Washington of DeRidder, Louisiana? They won their biggest case ever because of my investigative skills."

"Rosebud," Biggie said, "if bullshit was music, you'd be a brass band. Still and all, I know I can trust you. We make a good team—Willie Mae has the instincts, you have the imagination, and I have the brains. Between us we can solve this mystery."

"What do I have, Biggie?" I asked.

"Honey, you have the innocence of youth. We may need you most of all before this is over. Now, pour me a glass of water and let's get on with it."

"Biggie," I said, "I just thought of something. Remember when the mayor died and you put a tablecloth over him and stuck your head under there?"

"Of course I remember," Biggie said.

"Well, Biggie," I said, "somebody in that room was watching you do that—and they looked really mad."

"Who was it, honey?"

"I can't remember. . . ."

"Try, J.R. It may be important."

"I can't, Biggie. I can almost see um, but then I lose it. What did you do that for, anyway?"

"I was seeing if I could smell cyanide."

"Could you?"

"Not sure. It did smell kind of sweet and at the same time like your socks when you've been playing all day in them. Still, I just couldn't be sure. I think I know a way we can find out. That's why I stole that towel from the café." She turned to Rosebud. "Rosebud, are you familiar with Shreveport?"

"Miss Biggie, I know the state of Louisiana from north to south. Why, I was working the lights at the Louisiana Hayride when Elvis sang there back in the fifties."

"Good. What I want you to do is take that towel over to the Prudhomme Lab on King's Highway." She reached for her purse and pulled out the pill still wrapped in foil and handed it to Rosebud. "Take this one, too." She dropped the pill Elvaree had brought into his hand.

"Anything else?" Rosebud asked.

"Matter of fact, there is," she said, and pulled her hot-water bottle out of the drawer. "J.R., pour that milk shake in this. Now, you take that towel, the two pills, and this milk shake to Dr. Prudhomme. Tell him I think they might contain cyanide. Why don't you take that dog along, too? I've just got a funny feeling about that little feller. You tell Sol Prudhomme that Biggie Weatherford says hurry it up. I haven't got all the time in the world to deal with this murder. I've got to put on a Pioneer Days festival."

"When are you coming home, Biggie?" I asked.

"The day after tomorrow, honey. I've got a few more people I need to question, and this is the best place to do it. By the way, Willie Mae, do me a favor and make up a batch of your pecan pralines and take them over to Norman Thripp in the jail. Tell him I'm thinking of him."

14

Biggie came out of the hospital looking like she'd been on a long vacation.

"I feel like a girl again," she said.

That morning we all sat around the kitchen table while I helped Willie Mae make an angel food cake. She said I could sift the flour while she beat up a dozen egg whites.

"Miss Biggie," she said, "how come you want *angel food*? Seems to me like that'd be the *last* thing you'd want to eat." She waved the beater at me. "Watch out, boy! You wastin' flour all over the floor."

"I don't want to eat it, Willie Mae. You can carry it down to your church if you want to. I want to *smell* it."

"Biggie," I said, "I wouldn't want to hurt your feelings, but I sure am glad Willie Mae came here. I ain't never seen you bake a cake in my whole life."

"Haven't," Biggie said. "You *haven't* seen me bake a cake."

"That's what I said, Biggie. You never do bake cakes."

Biggie grinned. "You're not hurting my feelings, honey. I

just never was one for womanly virtues. Always preferred to be outside running with the boys when I was a girl. Then when I got older I just never did take to housework. When I die, they'll say, 'Biggie Weatherford never learned to bake a pie or a cake, but she sure had fun!' "

I leaned over and gave her a great big hug. "That's okay, Biggie," I said. "You're still the best grandmomma in the whole world."

Just then the back door slammed and Rosebud came in. He was wearing his black suit with a red-and-black-plaid shirt and a yellow tie. He had a red rose in his buttonhole.

"Where you goin', Rosebud?" I asked.

"I'm takin' my little sweet patootie down to LaVon's Bait Shoppe for some fried catfish. Why ain't you ready, cher?"

"On account of because you're two hours early. That's why. What's wrong with you, man?"

Rosebud looked at the clock on the wall. "Well, good goodness," he said, "dogged if you ain't right. I guess I just got home from Shreveport so late last night, I plumb lost track of the time."

"Pour you a cup of coffee and tell me what you found out," Biggie said.

"Miss Biggie, that there Dr. Prudhomme allowed as how he ain't got time to do no labbin' for you before early next week for sure. He say he be covered up with work on account of they having a rash of food poisoning over there due to a bad batch of oysters that come up from the Gulf."

Willie Mae started beating the flour into the cake, one spoonful at a time. When it was all in there, she took a little bottle out of the cabinet and poured something into the batter.

Biggie's head went up like a snapping turtle. "What's that smell?" she asked.

"What?" Willie Mae said. "Oh, you mean this here? That's flavorin' for the cake. Why you want to know?"

"Hand me that bottle." Biggie took a big sniff. "Cyanide. Willie Mae, are you trying to poison us?"

"Huh," Willie Mae said, "maybe you should've learnt a few things about cooking. This here's almond extract. It's used to flavor cooking, that's all."

"And it's always used in angel food cake?"

"Miss Biggie, everybody in the world knows that—'cept you, I guess."

Biggie put her head between her arms on the table. She was shaking real bad.

"Biggie!" I said.

When she looked up at me, I saw she was laughing like a double-jawed hyena.

"No," she said, "I'm not the only one. Chief Trotter doesn't know it either. Who'd have guessed it? Something as good as cake smelling like cyanide."

"Biggie, how'd you know what cyanide smelled like in the first place?"

"We used it when I was a girl on the farm to kill rats," she said. "Lost a perfectly good momma cat and all her kittens once from a poisoned mouse. After that, Papa took to using traps. He felt real bad about killing old Patches. I must have cried for a week. I guess that's why I'll never forget the smell of cyanide."

"So, Biggie," I said, "if the mayor was killed with cyanide, what about those pills, those epi—whatever?"

"I didn't say he was killed with cyanide, J.R., but there's a chance he might have been. It's a mystery. Either one might have got him. We'll know more when we get the report back from Dr. Prudhomme. Right now, I could eat a horse. What's for lunch, Willie Mae?"

"Just let me get finished with this cake and I'll fix y'all something," Willie Mae said.

After she got her cake out of the oven, Willie Mae got out the ham she'd baked for Sunday dinner and made me and Biggie some sandwiches and a big pitcher of lemonade for our lunch. We took them out on the front porch to eat. We hadn't got started good before Miss Mattie McClure drove up and parked her car in our driveway.

"Hidy, Mattie," Biggie said. "Who's managing the tearoom?"

"I got Michelle Meredith Muckleroy helpin' me until school starts." She took a little folding fan out of her purse and started in fanning herself. "Lordy mercy, it's hot," she said. "Used to be it'd be already cooled off by this time of year. It's in the Bible that in the latter days, the weather's gonna get all outta whack. I think we're in the latter days. Don't you, Biggie?"

"No, I don't, Mattie. What's wrong with you? It's only the first week of September." Biggie poured a glass of lemonade and handed it to her. "Now drink this and tell me what's going on. I hear your boyfriend's been incarcerated for conduct unbecoming to a servant of the people."

Miss Mattie bit her lip until I thought she'd bite right through. Finally she said, "It was just all a terrible mistake, that's all."

"Well, in the name of Sam Houston and all that's holy, get on with it," Biggie said.

"Okay, okay," Miss Mattie said. "It seems the day before the funeral, Dovie, you know, the city secretary, was doin' the books and she found some money had turned up missing. Well, she told the judge about it and, as you well know, there's always been bad blood between the courthouse and city hall, so the judge just right away decided—"

"Mattie, don't give me that," "Biggie said. "I know

Franklin Grimes. He must have had something to go on or he never would have suspected Norman."

"Well, he didn't suspect Norman right at first," Miss Mattie said. "It was when they checked down at the bank and found he had just deposited ten thousand dollars in his account no more'n a week ago. Well, that's when Mr. Smarty Pants Judge decided to issue a warrant and throw my poor Norman in the pokey."

"Where do you reckon Norman Thripp got ten thousand dollars, if he didn't steal it?" Biggie asked.

"I'm gettin' to that—well, not exactly *that.* But he didn't steal it and here's why!"

Biggie sighed. "Well, why, Mattie? I declare, your tongue is downright frolicsome today."

"It was just a big mistake, don'cha see. When Shade Mc-Glodney, the city attorney, got the auditors in from Center Point, they found out Dovie had misplaced a decimal in the salaries budget, throwing the balance off by ten thousand dollars—and it just so happened that Norman'd just deposited a check from the insurance company for his sister Alma's life insurance. You remember Alma?" Miss Mattie helped herself to a ham sandwich and took a big bite. "Oowee, this ham's good," she said. "Well, anyway, Alma lived up near Hot Springs—Hope, I think it was. She'd had to go in the rest home on account of she took Alzheimer's disease, and Norman, bein' her only living relative, had to take out a guardianship on her."

"Wasn't Alma the big one with all that frizzy blond hair?" Biggie asked.

"No, that was Clarice. Alma was the pretty one—married that railroad man from Arkansas, don'cha know. He died soon after and Alma just stayed on up there. That check was for the sale of her home." Miss Mattie picked up Booger, who had been rubbing against her legs, but he jumped back down again. She brushed at her skirt with her hands. "Well, just as you might imagine," she went on, "Norman is mad enough to chew splinters and he's threatening to sue the city and the judge and everybody else for just tons of money—and I don't blame him one little bit. The idea!"

Biggie poured some more lemonade in my glass. "More, Mattie?"

"Maybe just a tad. All this talking does tend to dry a person out. Anyway, Shade says, whether Norman stole any money or not, the city's still in trouble because they thought the money was there and it's not. He says, and here's the good part, they may have to close the new dump and turn the property back over to the Plummer estate!"

"What do you mean?" Biggie asked. "I thought the city bought the land."

"No, they didn't own it," Miss Mattie said. "What they had was one of those ninety-nine-year leases on the place. They'll just have to go back on the lease. Naturally, the Plummer heirs will make them fill up the hole."

"Well," Biggie said, "that's the best news I've had since Hecter was a pup. Now we can concentrate on the festival and finding out who's been blowing up cars and killing mayors around here."

Miss Mattie looked puzzled. "Killing mayors? Mayor Gribbons died from a heart attack. Now, Biggie, just because you've solved a crime or two in the past, don't go thinking everybody that dies has gone and got themselves murdered." She stood up. "Well I gotta go count the lunch receipts. That Meredith Michelle don't have much of a head for figures."

After Miss Mattie left I said, "Biggie, what are you going to do about the Daughters?"

"What about the Daughters?"

"You know, the signs and stuff you made to protest that dump."

"Oh, honey, I'll think of something. Oh, goody, here comes Mr. Crabtree. I need to talk to him about his costume for the parade."

Mr. Crabtree sat down on the steps and started fanning himself with his hat. "Hotter than hell's doorknob, Miss Biggie. Pardon my profanity, but this heat has sorely strained my sense of decorum."

"Speak your mind, Mr. Crabtree," Biggie said. "I've never been shocked by biblical references. J.R., go in and get Mr. Crabtree a glass so I can pour him some lemonade."

When I came out, she was telling him she'd had the pants from her grandaddy's World War I uniform altered.

"You'll look splendid, Mr. Crabtree. Just splendid!" she said.

Mr. Crabtree looked like the starch had all gone out of him—kind of like the way I feel when Biggie tells me to get dressed up and pass the cookies at a Daughters' meeting.

"Now," Biggie said, "you just drink this lemonade and relax while I tell you some more good news. You have been selected to perform an important function for the festival, one that has previously been reserved for our most prominent citizen, the mayor. You are going to be the star attraction at the most popular booth on the midway."

Mr. Crabtree perked up a little. "And what might that be, Miss Biggie?"

"The dunking booth," she said.

"The—er, the *dunking* booth?"

"Yes, honey. All you have to do is sit on a little platform and people throw—"

"Miss Biggie, I know how a dunking booth works. I am just unsure as to whether I am the man for the job. Perhaps Mr. Thripp would be better suited. . . ."

"Pooh!" Biggie said. "Norman Thripp wouldn't be near the draw you would. Besides, he wouldn't do it. Too afraid of messing up what little hair he has left."

I guess Mr. Crabtree knew he was licked. He picked up his hat and walked around back to his apartment. I felt sorry for him, but I sure was going to take a shot at knocking him into the water tank. I hoped he'd still be wearing Biggie's granddaddy's uniform and that old coonskin cap.

When he left Biggie said, "I declare, that Wade Hampton Crabtree looked like death chewing on a biscuit, didn't he?"

"Yes'm, I guess," I said.

Biggie stood and picked up the tray with our plates and glasses. She was grinning like a possum. "Remind me to give you plenty of money for the carnival," she said. "I want you to dunk that southern-fried hush puppy good and proper!"

15

The festival was only one week away, and the town was thinking of nothing else. The Rotary Club had sent all the way to Fort Worth for a banner to stretch across Main Street that read: JOB'S CROSSING PIONEER DAYS—WE-B-FUN.

Butch made floral arrangements out of plastic bluebonnets and Indian paintbrush and tied them to all the parking meters around the square with plastic red ribbon. All the stores redecorated their windows with antiques and old stuff like churns and washtubs and plows. Miss Mattie had a mannequin in the window of the tearoom dressed in her grandmother's wedding dress.

The Daughters decided to use the protest banners they'd made even though the dump was already filled in. Now they said H.O.G.F. Biggie said that meant Honor Our Grand Forefathers, because what were the Daughters about if not honoring their forefathers? Besides, it would be a shame to waste all the work they'd done painting those signs.

On Monday morning, I was sitting on Biggie's bed playing with Booger while she got ready to go downtown. Willie Mae came in with the mail.

"Looks like a letter from that there Dr. Prudhomme," she said.

"J.R., read it to me while I powder my nose," Biggie said.

I read: " 'Ma Chère, How my heart leapt when your man brought a parcel from you! My mind went back to that enchanted week we spent together in Hot Springs—nineteen forty-eight, it was. I have only to close my eyes and again I am there with you . . . the candlelight dinners . . . the walks through the autumn woods . . . falling to sleep in your—' "

"Give me that!" Biggie tried to grab the letter, but I was faster. I climbed to the top of her bureau and scrunched up by the wall so she couldn't reach me. I read on:

" '—arms. What could my love be sending me? I asked myself—perhaps a ham, fresh cured on her beloved farm—jars of jellies or preserves from the bounty of her orchard. Imagine my surprise when, tearing open its wrappings, I beheld a stale milk shake, a dirty towel, *a dead dog*!

" 'Beware, *mon amie*. Beware! Cyanide in large amounts was found in the carcass of the little dog and in the residue of the towel. The milk shake? Most puzzling. It contained large amounts of a drug known as ephedrine—used in the management of illnesses of the respiratory system. Again, I say, beware, my little lover of the mystery.

" 'When maistrie cometh, the god of love anon/ Beteth hise winges, and farewell!/ He is gone!" Your devoted servant, S. Prudhomme.' "

"Old fool!" Biggie said. "Put that letter on my dresser and let's get to town."

She took the paper sack of evidence I'd gathered behind the café and walked out the door. I followed.

"We'll walk," Biggie said. "It's a beautiful day."

It was that. The trees along both sides of the street were

turning yellow and orange and red. Colored leaves lay all over the ground except in Mrs. Moody's yard. She was busy raking them into piles and burning them. The smoke smelled good. The sky was blue as Jimmie Sue's eyes. " 'Morning, Essie," Biggie said.

" 'Morning, Biggie. 'Morning J.R.," Mrs. Moody said. "You find out who blew up Mr. Crabtree's car yet?"

"Don't have the faintest," Biggie said. "Not much to go on. Wait a minute. What are those on top of that pile of leaves over by the front porch?"

Mrs. Moody walked over and dug some white sheets of paper out of the leaf pile. "Just trash, I reckon," she said, handing them over the fence to Biggie. "My Lord, it's just pure-dee awful the way folks don't have respect for the property of others. Don't you think so, Biggie? They'll just throw their trash anywhere."

Biggie was studying the papers and didn't answer the question. "Looks like just notes for Crabtree's book about the pope—must have blown over here after the explosion. Pitch um back into the fire, Essie." She handed the papers to Mrs. Moody, then stopped. "Wait a minute. This one has something written on the back. 'P-t October seventh.' Hmmm, that's funny. Wonder what 'p-t' means."

"That's next week, Biggie," I said.

Biggie stuck the paper in her purse. "Come on, J.R.," she said. "We've got things to do. Ta-ta, Essie."

Biggie stopped at Codgill's Jewelers. "I'm going in to talk to Mr. Codgill," she said.

"Can I go sit by the courthouse and watch the squirrels?" I asked.

"Good idea," she said. "Just wait for me there."

When I got to the courthouse, that biker was sitting on the same bench he'd been sitting on when I first set eyes on him, only this time he was feeding peanuts to a squirrel. I tried not to look at him and made up my mind if he tried anything with me, I'd yell my head off until Chief Trotter came out of the police station and took him to jail.

Pretty soon, Biggie came across the street looking like she'd just snared the blue ribbon at a hog callin'.

"What did you find out, Biggie?" I asked.

"You'll find out soon, honey," she said. "I've got a few more squirrels to tree, and then you'll know."

I saw a shadow fall between us and looked up to see the biker standing next to us. He wasn't much taller than Biggie, which surprised me on account of I guess my imagination must of made him bigger than he actually was. His hair was red and kind of curly and just came down to his shirt collar. I looked down at his hands holding his big black helmet and, for the first time, noticed they were shaped exactly like Biggie's—only bigger.

"Excuse me, ma'am," he said, "but would you be Mrs. Fiona Wooten Weatherford?"

His voice was soft and reminded me of Mr. Crabtree's southern accent.

"I am, indeed, son. And who might you be?" Biggie said.

"My name is Paul-and-Silas Wooten. I believe I may be a relative of yours—from the Tennessee branch of the family."

"What did you say your name was?" Biggie asked.

"Paul-and-Silas, ma'am. My mother was a churchwoman and quite fond of the old songs. She particularly liked 'Give Me That Old-Time Religion,' which contains the line: 'It was good for Paul and Silas—' "

"I know the song," Biggie said. "What makes you think you're kin to me?"

Paul-and-Silas bowed to Biggie. "It's a long story, ma'am. Do you think I might buy you and the boy a cold drink at the café while we discuss it?"

Biggie looked at her watch. "I think we can spare the time," she said. Biggie marched across the street, ignoring Mr. Thripp, who was driving his car and had to slam on his brakes to keep from hitting her. The biker and I followed.

Biggie led us to a booth way in back. "Now, state your case, son," she said.

"May I call you Miss Biggie?" he asked. "It appears that you are affectionately known by that name here in your charming town."

"I don't care if you call me King Kong," Biggie said. "Just tell me why you think we could possibly be related."

"I know it's a shock, Miss Biggie. But you must not be dismayed by my fearsome persona. I am, in reality, a gentleman gone astray. I graduated, cum laude, from Vanderbilt University with a degree in classical languages."

"Well, you could have fooled me," Biggie said.

"Yes, ma'am. May I continue?"

"Please."

"After graduation from college, I was beset by a veritable barrage of tragic family events, which set me adrift in a sea of confusion."

"You talk funny," I said.

"I know. I can't seem to help it; when I try to speak in the vernacular of the people, it comes out all wrong. To continue, both my parents were tragically killed in a ballooning accident over Albuquerque."

"They must have been very brave," Biggie said.

"Oh, yes. Brave and adventurous," Paul-and-Silas said. "My father billed himself as the 'Colonel of the Clouds,' and wore a white suit and a goatee. The balloon was made in the shape of a mint julep. My sister lost her life while bungee jumping from a water tower. After that, I was alone in the world. That's when I lost my way."

"Poor boy," Biggie said. "Who wouldn't?"

"Yes, ma'am. So then I fell in with a bad crowd of ne'er-do-wells and wastrels. I won't bore you with the sad details of my descent. Suffice to say I wasted my inheritance on drugs, liquor, and women. One night, under the influence of all three, I was persuaded to have myself tattooed. Several designs were put forward, but fortunately, even in my befuddled state, I was able to remember the Wooten family crest and selected that as my permanent adornment. See?"

He stretched out his arm and showed Biggie the tattoo.

"That's all very well," Biggie said, "but what's it got to do with me? There must be plenty of Wootens in Tennessee. Undoubtedly, some are related to me."

"Miss Biggie, my great-great-grandfather was the son of James Royce Wooten, founder of this fine little town."

Biggie's hand shook as she picked up her coffee cup.

"Well," she said, "that would make a difference. Then tell me this, young man: Why have you been stalking Jimmie Sue Jarvis? No Wooten would do such a shameful thing."

Paul-and-Silas stared at Biggie. "Stalking? Me? Oh, no, Miss Biggie. If anyone has been stalked, it is I. The lovely Jimmie Sue had been flattering me with her attentions for quite some time before your police chief made it clear that I was to find companionship elsewhere."

"Then why would she say such a thing?" Biggie asked. "She claims to be afraid of you."

"Miss Biggie," he said, "it is my opinion that the young lady thrives on excitement. I believe her only interest in me was to add spice to her current romance with the chief."

"You may be right," Biggie said. "Jimmie Sue does tend toward the dramatic. So what are your plans, young man?"

He sighed. "I suppose I'll stay and enjoy your charming festival, then it's back to the open road for me."

"Why not settle down here?" Biggie asked. "You might find you like it."

"It's a charming thought, Miss Biggie—one that I might consider. Still, you do seem to have more acts of violence occurring than one might expect for such a sleepy little town."

"Oh, don't mind that," Biggie said. "We'll have these crimes solved in no time. By the way, being a stranger in town, you might just be able to help."

"In what way, ma'am?"

"Oh, just keep your eyes and ears open. In the meantime, why don't you come for dinner on Friday. Willie Mae is making fried chicken, I believe."

"I'd be more than honored, Miss Biggie." He stood up and touched his forehead. "Until Friday, then."

"What do you think, Biggie?" I asked after he'd gone. "Do you think he's telling the truth?"

"I'm not sure," Biggie said, "but the old Wooten intuition tells me he just might be who he claims. We'll see."

Just then Mr. Popolus come over to the table.

"More coffee?" he asked.

"Sure, Julius," Biggie said. "Why don't you join us? Business looks pretty slim right now."

Mr. Popolus poured two cups and brought them to the table. He looked at me. "How 'bout some opple pie à la mode?" he asked.

"Sure!" I said.

"Not on your life," Biggie said. "Popolus, bring him a small dip of vanilla ice cream. It'll be lunchtime before long."

When he came back to the table Biggie started in asking questions. "Julius, did you know the mayor was poisoned by your angel food cake? Or it may have been the whipped cream. Did you know that?"

"Oh, no. No!" Mr. Popolus said. "My food is pure—it is clean."

"I'm not saying it's not," Biggie said. "I'm only saying that *somebody* put cyanide in the old boy's favorite dessert. How many people knew he always ordered that?"

"Most, I guess," he said. "He used to make a beeg point of saying how they could all have their Popolus Pies, he'd take my angel food cake. He always had whipped cream on top, too."

"Was anyone in the kitchen besides you that night?"

"Only the judge. He came back to ask for an ashtray. He was going to smoke a cigar, and I did not have any out on the tables. I try to discourage smoking in my place—it distresses people nowadays."

"Anyone else you can think of?"

"No. Only . . ."

"Only what?"

"Before I got the judge his ashtray, I thought I heard something outside and went out to check. It was only the poor leetle doggie, I suppose. I fed him the scraps later. Oh, I still can't believe our mayor was poisoned in Popolus's café. It is so sad, all this!"

Biggie patted his hand. "Never mind, honey," she said. "None of it was your fault. Come on, J.R., we've got things to do."

16

The day before the festival, we drove out to the farm to pick up Monica so she could spend the night at our house.

"Why aren't you and Mr. Sontag going?" I asked Mrs. Sontag as she put a big plate of sugar cookies on the table.

Mrs. Sontag laughed. "Bless your heart, sonny," she said, "it's festival enough for me to watch the sun come up over them pines and listen to the rooster crow. Coye and me ain't never taken much interest in what goes on in town. We're obliged to you for taking Monica in so she can enjoy it, though."

Mr. Sontag stood in the kitchen doorway wiping his hands on his overalls and standing first on one foot and then the other.

"Coye, why don't you come on over here and sit down?" Biggie asked. "You're jumping around like a June bug on a hot griddle."

Mr. Sontag came and sat beside Biggie. "Miss Biggie," he

131

said, "they was a crew of men over at the Plummer place doing what they called percolation tests."

"They were making coffee?"

"No'm. What they was doing was drilling little holes in the ground."

"Hmmm," Biggie said.

"Yes'm, that's right—and then they wanted to know if they could come over here and percolate on your land."

"You told them no, of course."

"Yes'm. But they done it anyway. Must of come back at night on account of we never seen um, but the next day I seen a little bitty pile of dirt out in the pasture and when I went out and taken a look, there it was—a little old hole no bigger'n my thumb."

"This doesn't look good," Biggie said. "They know I won't lease, yet they're still testing my land. Now why do you suppose they'd want to do that?"

Mrs. Sontag got up and poured more coffee for the grownups. She set the coffeepot down with a bang. "Biggie," she said, "suppose somebody thinks you ain't gonna be here all that long. Ever think of that?"

"I'm thinking, Ernestine. I'm thinking," Biggie said.

"Who'll inherit this place when you die?"

"Well, J.R. Who else?" Biggie said. "Since Horace died, J.R.'s all the kinfolks I've got."

"Biggie," I said, "remember that letter from Dr. Prudhomme? Remember he said that milk shake from the hospital had some of that stuff—what was it?"

"Ephedrine, honey, same as the mayor was taking instead of his heart pills. I'm pretty sure somebody switched the mayor's pills to that ephedrine stuff because he had a bad heart—"

"And everybody thought you were in the hospital on account of your heart," I said. "Biggie, somebody's trying to kill you!"

"Let's see," Biggie said, "Jimmie Sue brought me the milk shake. She could have slipped the medicine in it, but Mattie McClure got it from the hospital cafeteria, so she could have done it, too."

"Or somebody that worked there," Mr. Sontag said. "Do you know anybody that works in that there cafeteria?"

"Biggie!" I said, "I just remembered something. What about Paul-and-Silas? He was out there that day. Remember?"

"I sure do remember," Biggie said, "and he's come here claiming to be a relation of mine. Not only that, but he's from the same part of the country that double-talking Crabtree came from. I just wonder if there might be a connection between those two."

"Miss Biggie"—Mr. Sontag was looking hard at her— " 'pears to me like you'd do well to watch yourself—and watch out after the boy here, too. Seein' as how he's the one to inherit right after you."

"You're mighty right, Coye," Biggie said. "And I aim to do that. Now come on, kids. We've got to get back to town. Somebody around here's mean enough to suck eggs and sneaky enough to hide the shells—and I mean to find out who it is!"

The next morning I knocked on the door of the guest room and hollered for Monica to get dressed and come downstairs, then I headed for the kitchen. I could smell Willie Mae's country-cured ham frying on the stove. I sat down at the table just as she was taking a pecan waffle off the iron.

"Set yourself down, J.R., and let me pour some of this here maple syrup over your waffle. Where's your little friend-girl?"

"Coming," I said. "Willie Mae, I hope you don't ever take a notion to go back to Louisiana. You're the best cook in the whole world."

"Humph," she said. "I stays when I stays, and I goes when I goes. Only the spirits knows when that time gonna be."

I took a big piece of waffle on my fork and stirred it around in the syrup, then I about jumped right out of my skin. A big shadow came on the wall opposite me and the room got darker. It looked like the Frankenstein monster was standing at our back door. My eyes must of been big as hubcaps when I looked around, because Rosebud, who was the one standing in the doorway, was bout to bust a gut laughing at me.

"You must be pure-dee antsy this morning, J.R. It ain't nothing but old Rosebud. Betcha ain't never seen nothing like this in your whole life. Right?"

He sure was right. He was wearing his Mardi Gras costume. The suit was made to look like Indian buckskin only it was yellow cloth—shiny, like satin. Fringe made out of sparkly red and purple ribbons hung from the arms and chest. Across the back he had a picture of a desert sunset made out of sequins and rhinestones. But the best part of all was his headdress. It was purple-dyed turkey feathers on a red-sequin band with white ermine tails hanging down over his ears. When he smiled the gold in his teeth reflected the colors of his costume.

Willie Mae looked proud as a preacher on Easter Sunday, but all she said was, "Put this towel over you before you eat, or you'll have syrup all over your fine self."

Monica came into the kitchen grinning. "Well, if it ain't the Indian what scalped me," she said.

Rosebud laughed without making any noise and slapped his knees. "Girl, you won't do," he said. "You just won't do!"

Biggie came through the door carrying our costumes for the parade. She gave Monica an old-timey dress that used to belong to Biggie's grandma, who was a little bitty woman.

It had a matching sunbonnet. I had to wear my daddy's old Davy Crockett suit because Biggie said none of her male forebears were small as me and, anyway, they'd all worn out their clothes while they were living. Biggie wore a red dress with yellow flowers all over it and a big straw hat.

"Where's Willie Mae's costume, Biggie?" I asked.

"And just what makes you think I want to go down there and mess with all that hoo-rawin'?" Willie Mae said.

"Oh—"

"And, anyway, ain't I had enough of dressin' up—livin' in south Louisiana pert near all my life? No sir, I reckon I'll just stay here and enjoy a little peace and quiet with y'all outta my hair."

Biggie looked at her watch. "Hurry up, younguns," she said. "Parade starts in forty-seven minutes."

After we dressed, we walked down to the fire station, where the parade was lining up. Paul-and-Silas was standing under a tree across the street, watching. When he looked at me, I thought I felt a rabbit hop over my grave.

"What do you think of him, Biggie?" I asked. "Do you think he's telling the truth?"

"I'm not sure," she said.

"Miss Biggie, I've seen his kind before," Rosebud said. "I once saved my employer from a fast-talking con man just like him. It was in Bayou Teche—"

"Never mind," Biggie said, "I won't be taken in by an impostor. Now, you three climb up in the wagon. They're lining up already. I've got to join the Daughters."

Just then, Judge Grimes came strolling up wearing a black frock coat with a string tie and black boots. He took off his hat and bowed low to Biggie.

"Biggie, you're a national treasure," he said. "In all my born days, I've yet to see such a lineup for our parade. How do you do it?"

Biggie smiled up at him. "Why thank you, Judge. I couldn't have done it alone. Lots of help, don'cha know."

"You're just modest, Biggie," he said. "I like that in a woman."

Monica giggled, but the judge ignored her. "One of these days," he said to Biggie, "I'm going to talk you into marrying me. You just don't know it yet."

Biggie actually blushed. "Shame on you, Franklin Grimes. We're both too old to be thinking like that."

"Mark my words, pretty lady, one of these days . . ."

Biggie laughed and started off toward the Daughters, who were gathered at the corner across the street.

Next year, no matter what Biggie says, I'm not riding in the parade. It's lots more fun to watch. Our wagon was lined up behind the cowboys from the rodeo, and their horses kept doing their business on the street. You can just imagine what the smell was like. Even worse, we were in front of the high-school band. The only songs they know are the school fight song and "Wipe Out." Those two sound exactly the same when played by the Fighting Turkey Band.

It was still ten minutes before starting time, so me and Monica slipped off to see the rest of the lineup. Jimmie Sue and Chief Trotter led the parade in the police car followed by the fire truck carrying all the town officials. Mr. Thripp was sitting right in front beside Chief Reynolds, where Mayor Gribbons used to ride. Mr. Thripp was wearing his Korean War navy uniform. Judge Grimes and all the county commissioners sat on top of the hoses and ladders in back. A banner hanging from the side read: IN MEMORIUM, OSBERT GRIBBONS, 1938–1995.

Next came the Center Point High School band in blue and silver uniforms. They made the Job's Crossing band look like dirt. They were playing "Washington Post March" real snappy. Behind them, the Mooslah Temple Shriners, in their little cars, rode around in circles on the street honking their horns and waving at the crowd. It's lucky for them they didn't have to be behind the horses on account of they were so close to the pavement.

The Daughters followed the Shriners, carrying their signs and singing "Deep in the Heart of Texas." Since they had to hold on to the signs, they couldn't clap at the clapping part, so they stomped their feet instead.

The floats followed next, my favorite being the FFA float. Ezell Washington's prize boar that he'd raised from a shoat was riding on the back of the flat-bed truck. The banner on the side read: I'M A HOG FOR PIONEER DAYS.

The rodeo cowboys came next, about twenty of them riding scrawny old cutting horses. They looked about as dilapidated and bored as their horses. Me and Monica and Rosebud and Mr. Crabtree followed in the wagon.

We were followed by the Homecoming Queen and the FFA Sweetheart sitting on the backs of open convertibles loaned for the day by the Buick dealer.

Butch brought up the rear in the gypsy costume Willie Mae had dug up for him. He had on a red skirt with a white blouse and silver bangles jingling around his ankles. He was wearing Willie Mae's dragon shawl and carrying a stick with colored ribbons tied to it. I'm pretty sure he had more fun than anybody, dancing along and waving his stick. He sure looked a lot prettier than Essie Spurlock, the FFA Sweetheart.

After the parade broke up, the people wandered over to the vacant lot across from the courthouse to buy cold drinks and hot dogs and to visit the attractions. The carnival had set up along one side; the music from the merry-go-round sounded real pretty. After we'd gone home and gotten out of our costumes, I went into Biggie's room. Biggie was soaking her feet.

"Lordy mercy, I'm tired," she said. "My feet feel hotter than a two-dollar pistol."

"Biggie," I said, "can me and Monica go down to the square and get a hot dog for lunch?"

"Sure, honey," she said. "I'm fixing to take me a good rest this afternoon, then I'll come down there after supper to take in the calf scramble and the cute-baby contest. Y'all kids be careful, now. You hear?"

17

What do you want to eat?" I asked Monica.

"How about cotton candy and a caramel apple?" she said.

"Well—I don't know. Biggie likes for me to eat a balanced diet. I may just have a hot dog for now."

Monica hit me on the shoulder. "Yeah! Right!" she said. "Like a weenie made out of cottonseed meal and red dye is gonna make you grow big and tall! Oh, well, come on. We can have cotton candy for dessert."

When we got to the hot-dog booth, you'll never guess who was working there—Jimmie Sue! She had on tight white shorts and a blue baseball cap with *Fighting Turkeys* on the front. Her ponytail looked real pretty sticking out the back. A lot of guys were hanging around trying to hit on her, but when she saw us, she smiled real big.

"Hey, J.R.," she said. "Who's your little friend?"

Monica said, "My name's Monica Sontag and I was left too close to the fire when I was a baby. That's why I just have half my hair."

"Shoot! I didn't even notice," Jimmie Sue said. "What can I get for you?"

"I'll have the foot-longer with chili, a pack of Fritos, and a root beer," Monica said.

"Make mine a corny dog," I said, "and fries."

We found a bench under a tree and sat down to eat our lunch.

"Who are those two old people holding hands over by the Ferris wheel?" Monica asked.

I looked and saw Norman Thripp and Miss Mattie, pussy-footing along like they were the only two people on the face of the earth. I told her who they were.

"Wouldn't that just rattle your cat," Monica said. "I thought only young people fell in love. Them two look like they was stuck together with Super Glue."

"I know," I said. "Makes you sick, don't it?"

Monica stuck her finger down her throat and pretended to barf on the ground.

We finished our lunch then decided to walk around and check out all the booths and rides.

"Hey, I gotta idea," Monica said. "How 'bout we go over and look at old Ezell Washington's prize boar? I bet I could raise one that good if Daddy'd only let me. He wants to make bacon out of um before they're hardly big enough to grunt."

The boar was displayed in a pen next to the taco stand, which was being run by Mr. Peoples, who was sitting out in front playing his guitar and singing "Mule Train."

"Hidy, J.R.," he said. "Y'all want a taco?"

"Eee-yew," Monica said. "Who could eat a taco with that hog smell all around here?"

"I know," said Mr. Peoples. "I ain't sold a one. I can't even bring um in with my pickin' and singin'."

I felt sorry for Mr. Peoples, so I bought a snow cone from

him, but it tasted like hog so I threw it away after we got out of sight.

"What do you want to do now?" Monica asked after she'd admired that hog a good long while.

"The dunking booth," I said. "I need to practice my throw."

We walked over to the dunking booth, which was right next to Jimmie Sue's hot-dog stand. Chief Trotter was sitting on the hot seat. He told us Mr. Crabtree's shift wouldn't begin until after the rodeo.

"Reckon I oughta try to knock the chief off?" I asked.

"Shoot yeah. Why not?" Monica said. "Might give you some practice for tonight when you soak that there old Mr. Crabtree."

I plopped down my dollar. "Six balls," I said.

Meredith Michelle Muckleroy was taking the money. "I hope you hit him," she said. "I'm tired of standing here all day taking people's money and watching everybody miss by a country mile."

I did my dead-level best but didn't even come close, so I bought six more balls and shot off another round. Still no luck. Chief Trotter was grinning from one ear to the next.

"Shoot, J.R.," Monica said, "you look frustrated as a banty rooster in a pen full of geese. Let's go on over to Biggie's house. You can toss me a few balls to get warmed up for tonight."

"Maybe you're right," I said. "A little practice is just what I need."

We went back to the house and found Biggie and Willie Mae sitting on the front porch. Biggie looked real serious.

"J.R.," she said, "ordinarily I don't worry about you running around Job's Crossing by yourself—"

"I know, Biggie," I said.

"But murder suspects are getting common as pig tracks around here."

"Yes'm. I know that, too." I sat down on the steps next to Biggie.

"What I'm saying, J.R., is, I want you and Monica to be especially careful at the carnival tonight." She put her hand on my head, and I could feel it shaking. "You kids stay where the crowds are—and don't you dare go near any dark or secluded places. You hear?"

"Yes'm. Has something happened we don't know about?"

Biggie took off her glasses and wiped them on the hem of her dress.

"Not exactly," she said. "Nothing has what you call *happened*, but I've been thinking about what we already know, and until we catch our killer, you might as well be walking into a tiger's cage with a hamburger in one pocket and a hot dog in the other."

"Why would anyone want to hurt J.R., Miss Biggie?" Monica asked. " 'Pears to me like you're the one that better be watchin' your back."

"I am, Monica," Biggie said. "But if they go after me, and they've tried already, they'll still have to get J.R. first before they can get at my land." She shook her head. "Maybe you ought not go tonight."

"Biggie! I've *gotta* go tonight! I've been waiting all summer for this—and helping you, too, don't forget. You just can't make me miss all the fun, Biggie. You just can't!"

"And, Miss Biggie, he's got to knock Mr. Crabtree in the water," Monica said. "Only reason we came home now was so I could give him a little coachin' in the pitchin' department."

I let that pass. "Puleeze, Biggie!" I said. "We'll be the carefullest two people you've ever seen!"

"Oh, all right," she said. "But just remember, if anything happens to you I'll never forgive myself."

I got out my catcher's mitt and me and Monica spent the rest of the afternoon warming up my throwing arm. I got to where I could hit a buzzard's eye in the rain.

"I'm gonna get him tonight, for sure," I said. "You just be makin' up your mind which one of them teddy bears you want me to win you."

"I don't want a teddy bear," Monica said. "I want one of them hats they put your name on. That's what I want."

Rosebud was watching from the back steps. Me and Monica went over and took a seat beside him.

"What do you think, Rosebud?" I asked. "Think I can take him?"

"Reckon so," he said, "if you just pay attention and keep your eye on that little spot you got to hit and don't be thinkin' about how he's gonna look splashin' around in that there water tank. Concentration. That's the key."

"I'm kindly hungry," Monica said. "Reckon when supper's gonna be ready?"

"It's ready now, youngun," Willie Mae said from the back door. "Y'all get in here and wash your hands. I think I hear Paul-and-Silas at the door now."

Unbeknownst to us, Biggie had also invited the judge for supper. When we got to the dining room, they were already sitting down. Willie Mae had put one of Biggie's white damask cloths on the table. The chicken-fried steak was served on Biggie's china platter with the gravy in a little gravy boat on the side. Willie Mae had made mashed potatoes with rivers of butter floating on top and black-eyed peas cooked with ham hocks. A basket with a napkin on top held Willie Mae's hot biscuits. We had tomato aspic for a salad. A big bowl of roses from the garden sat smack-dab in the middle of the table.

"Oo-wee," Monica said, "y'all eat *good* around here!"

"Miss Biggie," Paul-and-Silas said, "I feel like I'm back home in Tennessee at my poor dead mother's table."

I wasn't thinking about food. I was wondering whether or not I was about to get me a new granddaddy. The judge was looking at Biggie like she was good enough to eat. I gotta admit, that thought didn't appeal to me. I didn't say much during supper. Monica couldn't say a whole lot on account of her mouth being so full of food, but Biggie and the grown-ups didn't seem to notice due to the fact that they were talking their heads off about the coal leasing and what could be done to stop it.

As soon as we got through helping Willie Mae clear the table I said, "Can we go now, Biggie?"

Before she could answer, someone knocked on the door and Willie Mae went to answer it. She came back in the room followed by Miss Mattie and Mr. Thripp, Miss Lonie Fulkerson and Jimmie Sue.

"Travis couldn't come," Jimmie Sue said. "The crowd's got so big down at the midway he had to deputize Butch to help him keep order. A Shriner drove one of those little cars right into the penny-pitching booth!"

"That'll be fine," Biggie said. "With the two children, Willie Mae, and Mr. Crabtree, we'll have eleven."

"Where is old Crabtree, anyway?" Monica asked.

"He's up in his room pouting over having to man the dunking booth tonight," Biggie said. "Willie Mae, tell Rosebud to go upstairs and fetch him."

"What's this all about, Biggie?" the judge asked.

"Why, honey, Willie Mae is going to conduct a séance. It's a last resort. I want her to raise the spirit of Osbert Gribbons so I can ask him what he knows about the low-down rotten polecat that mailed him a one-way ticket to the Great Beyond."

"Now, Miss Biggie, I'm not real fond of the idea of disturbing the dead," Mr. Thripp said.

"What if we get a wrong number and call forth Jack the Ripper—or Hitler?" Miss Mattie said. "Ooh, I'm getting goose pimples."

"Or Dracula," Jimmie Sue said. "What would we do then?"

"Dracula's a *fictional* character," Monica said. "I don't think you could call him."

The judge spoke up. "Biggie, I think this is a damn foolish idea, and I don't mind saying it. But if it's what you want to do, well, let's get started."

"I'm here, Miss Biggie," Mr. Crabtree said from the doorway, "but I don't quite understand . . ."

Biggie wasn't listening to any of them; she had been busy drawing the drapes and turning off all the lights. Now she was putting two candles on the table, one on either side of the bowl of roses.

Willie Mae came into the room wearing her dragon shawl over her head and sat in the center of one long side of the table directly in front of the flowers. She waved her arms for everyone else to take a seat.

A voice spoke out in the darkness.

"Biggie, I thought you thed we were invited here for thum more of Willie Mae'th good thugar cookieth."

"Quiet, Lonie," Biggie said. "We'll have cookies and coffee after we're through. Now, all join hands."

Willie Mae closed her eyes and started in humming sort of low and spooky. I sneaked a look around the table and caught the judge's eye. He winked at me. Suddenly, Willie Mae let out a holler and started shaking like a wet dog then jerked her hands free and began waving them slowly over the flowers.

Directly Jimmie Sue said, "What was that?"

145

I felt it, too. It was a cold feeling, like a breeze, only not exactly—more like when you walk outside on a real still, cold day.

Next, I saw mist rising up out of the bowl of roses, slow at first, then more, until a fog seemed to cover up the whole tabletop and swirl all around our heads. I could hear water, too, gurgling like a stream running over rocks.

A voice spoke out of the darkness, not from any one spot, but from all around us.

"Who calls?"

"It's me," Willie Mae said. "I call from the corporal world to the world of spirit. Who you?"

"The spirit of Osbert Gribbons. Why do you disturb my rest?"

Jimmie Sue screamed and tried to get up, but the judge kept a tight hold on her hand.

Biggie spoke. "We want to know who killed you," she said. "Tell us what you know, Osbert Gribbons."

"It's nice to know you remembered me," the ghost said. "How are all my constituents? Do they speak of me often?"

"Yes, yes," Biggie said. "We even named a parade after you. Now, tell us who bumped you off, Osbert. We don't have all night."

"Hurry up," Willie Mae said. "The spirits can't last long in this here atmosphere."

"Well, let me think," the ghost said. "First, somebody switched my pills on me, not a nice thing to do to a man with a diseased heart, let me tell you—"

"Who?" said the judge. "Tell us who did this to you, Osbert."

"Yeth," said Miss Lonie. "Don't keep uth in thuthpenth."

"And that cake tasted funny," Mayor Gribbons's ghost said, "or maybe it was the whipped cream. Yes, I believe it was the whipped cream. After that, all I remember is rising

146

above my body and watching you all from above. That wasn't very nice of you to lift me up by my hair, Biggie—not dignified, don'cha know."

"Tell us more about the cake," Jimmie Sue said.

"I can't," the voice said. "I'm getting weaker . . . weaker . . . I'm fading away."

Suddenly, a loud voice said, *It was somebody in this room!*

We all sat still for a minute, too spooked to talk, then Biggie got up and turned on the lights.

"What do you know about that?" she said. "Somebody right here in this room!"

18

Biggie made me and Monica stay around while Willie Mae served coffee and cookies in the living room. Of course they were all talking at once about the séance and how they never would of believed a person could be brought back from the dead if they hadn't seen it with their very own eyes.

The judge puffed on his cigar and said he thought trickery was involved on account of he had a analytical mind and, given time, he'd be able to figure out what Willie Mae did to put one over on us. I'd sure hate to be in his shoes. Willie Mae gave him a look that would freeze a cat when he said that. Jimmie Sue said it was the most exciting thing she'd ever seen, and they'd never believe her down at the courthouse when she told them about it tomorrow. Mr. Thripp didn't say much, but I saw his hand shaking as he held his coffee cup.

"I thought he seemed at peace. Didn't you think he seemed at peace, Lonie?" Miss Mattie said.

"I thought he theemed thpooky," Miss Lonie said. "He gave me gooth bumpth."

"Well," Mr. Thripp said, "I, for one, resent him saying it was someone in this room. The very idea! Suggesting that one of us might be a murderer."

"One of *you*," Mr. Crabtree said. "I wasn't there that night."

"Me neither," Jimmie Sue said. "Remember? I had an asthma attack."

"That doesn't mean one of you couldn't have sneaked into the café kitchen and slipped something into the whipped cream," the judge said, "that is if there was anything in the whipped cream—and we only have a phony ghost's word for that."

"Not so, honey," Biggie said. "I sent a sample off to a lab to be analyzed. There was cyanide in the whipped cream all right."

Mr. Thripp stood up. "Well," he said, "I've heard enough. Come on, Mattie. The rodeo starts in thirty minutes."

"I've gotta be going, too," Jimmie Sue said. "Gotta get back to the hot-dog booth. Can I give you a ride, Mr. C.?"

"Thank you, my dear," Mr. Crabtree said, "but since my ordeal doesn't begin until after the rodeo, I believe I'll just rest in my quarters a little longer. Miss Biggie, thank you for an—er, interesting evening."

"I must go, too," the judge said, putting out his cigar. "Thanks for a fine dinner, Biggie. I hope you'll forgive an old lawyer his skepticism."

"Not at all, honey," Biggie said.

When they'd all gone, Rosebud came out of the kitchen showing all his gold teeth. "How'd I do, Miss Biggie?" he asked.

"Honey, you deserve an Oscar for that performance."

"Well, if that don't beat old Billy," Monica said. "You mean this here was all just a show?"

"Sure was, honey," Biggie said, "and a ring-tailed tooter

of a show it was. Every single one of them was taken in."

"But that mist. I saw it; it was all over the room," I said. "I thought it was Mayor Gribbons floating around."

"Dry ice," Willie Mae said. "When I was wavin' my hands over the flower bowl, I just dropped a few chunks in the water. Didn't you hear it bubbling?"

"I did," Monica said. "But, listen. I know that voice was coming from all around us. How'd you do that, Rosebud?"

Biggie picked up a cookie and took a big bite. "That was easy. Rosebud hid little speakers in all four corners of the room and talked through a microphone from the spare bedroom."

"Rosebud!" I said. "Shoot, Biggie, Rosebud don't sound anything like Mayor Gribbons."

"That's what you think, little man," Mayor Gribbons's voice said. It was so real I like to jumped out of my skin.

"How'd you do that, Rosebud?" I asked.

"Why, son, I'm known all over the Gulf Coast as the Man of Many Voices. I did a one-man show on the *Delta Queen* for two whole years. They begged me to stay on, but an disfortunate event during a card game after the show forced me to jump ship."

Then I remembered something. "Biggie," I said, "what happened to Paul-and-Silas?"

"He left right after the séance, honey," Biggie said. "I guess he must have had something on his mind."

"Can we go now?" Monica said. "I've got a strong hankering to get back down to that there carnival."

"I suppose so," Biggie said, "but remember what I said, and watch yourselves. I saw something during the séance that has made me even more fearful for all our safety. That killer is like a scorpion with his tail up now that we've showed our hand. Anything can happen."

"What, Biggie? What'd you see?" I asked.

"Something that surprised me a great deal—but I'm not ready to tell you yet. I need more evidence. You two kids just go on, but be extra careful. You hear?"

"Yes'm."

"Do you want to go to the rodeo?" I asked Monica when Biggie finally let us out of the house.

"Naw. Let's go to the midway. I want to see them pickled baby pigs they got in them jars." Monica stopped and grabbed hold of my hand. "J.R., I heard some of 'em say they had real human babies in that place—put up just like my mama's bread-and-butter pickles—and they'd let you look at them if you'd pay them another two dollars."

"Ee-yew. What you wanta see that for?"

"I don't know," she said, "it just makes me kind of shivery thinking about it."

It was good and dark by then, and a full moon was just rising up over the pecan trees around the courthouse. A breeze ruffled Monica's hair on her good side, and she looked right pretty if you didn't look too close. I decided to humor her. We could hear the music from the merry-go-round as we entered the grounds between two tents. We headed for the freak tent first.

"You go on in," I said. "I believe I'll sit this one out."

Monica gave her money to a little dark man with three fingers missing and disappeared inside the tent. I threw some balls at some fake milk bottles while I waited. It was rigged, of course. I hit those bottles twice, and they just popped right back up again like they was on springs.

"I'm a personal friend of Chief Trotter of the Job's Crossing Police Department," I told the old woman that took my money, "and I might just turn you in for running a crooked game."

"Yeah, right," she said, and started in hollering for folks to step right up and win a giant panda.

When Monica came out, she said the pig was the real thing, but the pickled baby wasn't nothing but a plastic baby doll in a jar.

"I coulda seen something that'd rattle your knickers for sure if I'd of had another three dollars," she said.

"Yeah, what?" I said.

"Well," she said, "they had this guy in there—at least he looked like a guy with a wig on, and he was wearing a ladies' bathrobe."

"So?"

"Shut up and listen," she said. "I'm trying to tell you, ain't I? Anyway, this guy, or whatever he was, said he was a her—hermorpha—something, and if we'd pay another three dollars he'd go in the back room and show us he had a man's thing and a woman's, too! You believe that, J.R.?"

"Heck, no. There's no such of a thing as that. What's wrong with you, Monica? I bet if you'd had the money, you'd of gone in there, too!"

Monica grinned kind of sheepish. "Well—I might of," she said. "What you reckon we oughta do next?"

"Rides!" I said. "I been dyin' to get on that big hammer-lookin' thing that turns you upside down."

"I ain't gettin' on that thing," Monica said. "I aim to hold on to that there good dinner Willie Mae cooked for us. How 'bout we get on the Ferris wheel?"

"Okay," I said. "But you gotta promise we'll ride the hammer thing later."

As it turned out, we never got to ride the hammer thing, but I had all the excitement I could use that night without it.

It was real neat when the Ferris wheel stopped with us on top. We could look down and see the whole town.

"Look, there's y'all's house," Monica said. "See, there's the garage apartment and Biggie's car sitting right out front.

And looky there. I see Biggie and some of her old-lady friends playing bingo just right under us."

"Monica, stop wiggling around so much," I said. "You're gonna tip us over."

I was watching the dunking booth. A big crowd had gathered, most of them waiting to take a stab at giving Mr. Crabtree a bath. It wasn't hurting Jimmie Sue's business a bit; lots of folks were buying hot dogs to eat while they waited.

That biker, Paul-and-Silas, was sitting on his bike watching everything from the edge of the crowd.

"What next?" Monica wanted to know.

"How 'bout we go get in line to dunk Crabtree," I said. "I'm getting scared somebody's gonna beat me to him."

"Ooh, just one more ride," Monica begged. "Come on, J.R., please!"

"Okay," I said. "Which one?"

"How 'bout the swings?"

"How 'bout the Tilt-A-Whirl?"

"Okay, the Tilt-A-Whirl, but I warn you, I'm gonna scream my head off."

And she did. My head was buzzing from her squealing in my ear by the time that ride was over and we were making our way through the crowd toward the dunking booth.

"Hey, y'all," Jimmie Sue hollered when she saw us. "I got a special on foot-longers, just for you two."

Monica wanted to get one, but I had to pass. My stomach was still going 'round and 'round like that Tilt-A-Whirl. Anyway, the crowd had thinned, and it was time for me to take my shot.

I felt kind of bad there for a minute when Mr. Crabtree grinned at me and gave a little wave, but then I remembered how he'd lied to Biggie and pretended to be someone he wasn't just so he could get a lease on her land, and I fired off the first ball. It missed by a country mile and bounced off the side of the tent.

I shut my eyes and remembered what Rosebud had said: Concentrate on the target, not the man. This time I came closer; the ball bounced off the side of the tank.

"You can do it, J.R. Just take your time, like I taught you," Monica said.

I wound up and got off the third shot. The ball went wild, but then a strange thing happened. Mr. Crabtree got a real funny look on his face and then just slowly started to roll off the seat and into the water. it was like one of those slow-motion movies. He sank like a rock. Monica and I just stared for what seemed like a long time but must of been no more than a few seconds. Monica screamed. Then I noticed the water in the tank turning red. Real red.

"Come on!"

I grabbed Monica by the hand, and we ran around behind the tent, then stopped—dead still. I couldn't believe what my eyes saw. There was Jimmie Sue ducking through the flap in back of the hot-dog tent. But it was what she was holding in her hand that made my heart pound like a rock in a hubcap. It was one of those skewers they roast the weenies on—and it was dripping with blood. Just as she slipped inside, she gave us a look that I'll never forget as long as I live. It was pure-dee evil.

That's the last thing I saw, because the very next thing I knew, someone had thrown a sack over my head and I felt myself being carried down the alley behind the vacant lot. Monica screamed, then was silent. I heard running feet behind us.

The last thing I remember hearing was Jimmie Sue shouting, "Help! Somebody get over here. A man's been stabbed!"

19

I knew there had to be two men, because one of them carried Monica and the other carried me down the alley where they calf-roped us and threw us in the bed of a pickup truck. They never said a word to us or each other, just jumped in the cab and drove away, fast.

As soon as we took off, I scrunched myself over close to Monica.

"You okay?" I asked.

"No, I ain't okay, J.R.," she said. "I've just been hog-tied and kidnapped. Where you reckon they're takin' us?"

"Let me see if I can get this tow sack off my head," I said.

I wriggled around until I got my head loose then inched my elbow onto the wheel section and raised myself up so I could peer over the edge of the truck bed. It was almost light as day due to the moon being full that night.

"I just saw the water tower go by," I said. "That means we're on Abe Hawkins Road. Monica, that means we're headed toward your house!"

"Can you tell who they are?"

"Naw, can't raise myself up that high," I said.

"Well, do you recognize the truck?"

"Uh-uh. It's old, though, and green, I think."

"J.R., I'm scared."

"Don't worry," I said. "Just keep your head down and pretend you're passed out or something. We don't want them to take the notion we've recognized them. I'm gonna see if I can get back under this sack."

Monica scooted over close to me. "J.R., do you think they might be gonna—I can't say it."

"Naw. Shoot, Biggie'll find us."

I wished I could believe that. How would Biggie find us? Heck, how would she even know we were missing in that crowd?

The truck turned onto a bumpy old dirt road.

"Ow!" Monica said.

"Shhh, they might hear you. Just make out like you're bouncing on a trampoline."

"Some trampoline," Monica said in a grumpy voice.

The road got bumpier and me and Monica got as close together as we could to keep from bouncing all over the place.

"Where you reckon we are now, J.R.?" Monica panted. "I can't take much more of this."

Just then the truck stopped, and we heard both doors slam. I peeked out from under the sack, but the moon had gone under a cloud, making it as dark as a bucket of black cats. All I could make out was the shape of pine trees against the sky, which didn't help a whole lot on account of Kemp County's just about all growed up in pine trees.

The two men didn't say a word, just pulled us out of the truck. I could hear their feet rustling through the dry leaves as they carried us away from the truck. Then suddenly, I felt myself flying through the air—but not for long. Before you could say "Remember Goliad!" I hit the ground. Then Monica came flying by and landed with a grunt beside me.

The next sound I heard was the pounding of feet over our heads as they ran back to the truck and sped off.

I sat up and looked around then stretched as much as possible, seeing I was still trussed up like a hog. My head must of hit a rock, because I could feel a little trickle of something I thought must be blood running down my cheek. I wiped it on my sleeve.

"Monica," I said, "you okay?" My voice sounded loud in the still night.

She didn't answer.

"Monica!" I tried inching over toward where I'd heard her land. We seemed to be in some kind of hole or ditch. The ground around us was covered with rocks and pine needles.

"Oow! Oh—ouch!"

"Where are you?"

"Over here. I think I've broken my leg. Oh, it hurts!"

I struggled with my ropes until I got my hands loose, then, quick as I could, untied my legs and crawled over toward Monica's voice.

"Gimme your hand," I said. I reached in the direction her voice had come from until I felt the tips of her fingers, then slid toward her. I put my arm around her, even though I don't really care much for touching girls.

"Be still, now," I said. "I'm going to untie you."

When I got her ropes loose, I felt for her leg and, when I did, I wanted to cry. It was sticking out from under her at an angle no leg ought to be in, and when I pressed on it, I felt the bone move. Now she was sobbing kind of like a baby kitten.

"Wait," I said. "I'll make you a bed."

I started raking pine needles into a pile with both hands and pushing them toward her. "Now," I said, "try to lie down in this and relax while I try to straighten out your leg."

She hollered a lot, but I finally got her as comfortable as I could under the circumstances.

"I'm going to leave you for a minute," I said, "while I try to find out where we are."

It didn't take me long to discover we were in a big hole of some kind. The sides were steep, and red clay—damp and slick as ice. I tried to get a foothold to climb out but just kept sliding back to the bottom. Finally I gave up and came back to Monica.

"We'll just have to wait 'til daylight," I said. "Try to get some sleep."

"I can't sleep, J.R.," she said. "What if there's snakes in here—or black widows?"

I wished she hadn't of said that, because I hadn't thought of it, but I said, "They won't bother you if you leave them alone. Now, relax."

"I'll try," she said, "if you'll hold my hand."

I took hold of her hand and laid back and closed my eyes. All I could think of was that Biggie was in trouble. If they'd captured us, they sure would be going after Biggie. What if she was already dead and they were just waiting until morning to kill us, too? All this over some coal under Biggie's land. Why hadn't she just given them their leases?

Suddenly Monica sat up. "Listen," she said. "You hear that?"

"What?"

"It's a motor of some kind. Hear it, now?"

I sat up and listened as hard as I could. "It's nothing but cicadas in the trees," I said. "Go to sleep."

"Listen!" she said again.

"Oh, yeah," I said, "I hear it now. Sounds like a motorcycle. Oh, my gosh! A motorcycle!"

"You think it's that Paul-and-Silas guy?"

The motorcycle was getting closer. We heard a cracking noise like it had run over a stick.

"Help!" Monica yelled. "Get us out of here!"

I put my hand over her mouth. "Be quiet! What if he's one of them coming back to check on us?"

Now the engine stopped, and we could hear somebody crashing around in the brush over our heads. I squeezed Monica's hand tight, willing her to be quiet. Pretty soon we heard him get back on his bike and leave.

"Boy, that was close," I said. "How's your leg?"

"I can move it a little," she said. "Maybe it's not broken, after all."

All of a sudden, the moon came out and brightened the place up some. I looked around.

"Monica," I said. "I think we're in that hole Buster fell into. Look! There's that pile of brush we put down for him to climb up on."

"We can get out!" Monica said. "We can go to my house." She started to get up, then let out a yell. "Ow—J.R., I can't walk."

"That's okay. Can you stay here while I go for help?"

"No! Please! Oh, please don't leave me here, J.R. I might get snakebit."

"Well, we can't stay here forever."

"I know, but can't you just wait 'til daylight? It must be near sunup already."

I argued, but she seemed like she'd bust a gut if I left, so I agreed to stay.

"Might as well lie down and try to get some rest," I said.

"Okay, J.R.," Monica said, "but first I've got to tell you

something. You know those guys that tied us up and brought us out here?"

" 'Course."

"One of um was the judge."

"You're crazy," I said.

"No, really, J.R. You wants know how I know?" She didn't wait for me to answer. "How I know is, he smelled just like those old cigars the judge smokes—you know, kinda sweetish. Not only that, but I felt his old cigar case in his pocket while he was carrying me. And it *could* have been him, because Mayor Gribbons's ghost said it was somebody in that room."

I started to remind her that Mayor Gribbons's ghost never had been in that room, that it had been Rosebud doing the talking, and he didn't know any more than we did about who the murderer was. But I had more important things to think about, like how we were going to get word to Biggie before it was too late—if it wasn't too late already. I wondered if Biggie knew about the judge, or about Jimmie Sue killing old Crabtree with a weenie skewer.

I decided to let Monica in on what I was thinking.

"But why did the judge grab us?" she said. "Looked to me like he was doing a pretty good job of slinging his noose around Biggie anyway. Wouldn't it be easier just to marry her?"

"Oh, I don't know, Monica. I don't understand all I do know about this mess. All I know is, Biggie may be in trouble, and if I go to warn her, I'll have to leave you here, and if I stay here with you it may be too late."

I lay back down on the pine needles. "Well, the sun should be up in an hour. I'll stay with you that long, then I've got to go for help."

I must of dozed off because I dreamed I heard Biggie's voice.

"J.R.—J.R., where are you?"

I sat up and rubbed my eyes. "Biggie?"

Then I heard Rosebud's voice. "Where you be, boy?"

"Biggie!" I yelled, "Rosebud! Here we are. Down here!"

Monica started yelling, too. "Help! Here we are. Help!"

All of a sudden, I saw the most beautiful sight of my whole life. Biggie's face appeared over the edge of the pit. A moment later, Rosebud and Willie Mae came up behind her.

"J.R.," Biggie said, "can you get out, honey?"

"I can, but Monica's hurt her leg."

I climbed up the brush pile as far as I could, then Rosebud reached down and pulled me the rest of the way. Next, he climbed down himself and came back carrying Monica in his arms.

I remember getting scared again because I thought I heard the motorcycle coming back. After that, Rosebud said I passed out.

The next thing I remember is waking up in Biggie's big bed. Biggie was sitting next to me putting ice on my head. Monica was lying on the daybed against the wall with her foot propped on a pillow.

"Ouch," I said. "My head hurts!"

"No wonder," said Monica, "you've got a knot as big as a hickory nut."

"Just lie back and rest," Biggie said. "You've got something to tell your grandchildren. You can tell them all about the time you were kidnapped and almost killed."

"Ain't it the truth?" Rosebud said as he came into the room. "Even old Rosebud can't tell a tale like that."

"I wish I could remember it," I said.

"I remember," said Monica. "The judge and another man grabbed us at the carnival and threw us in the pit. We spent the night there, and Biggie and Rosebud and Willie Mae rescued us."

"Oh, yeah, it's all coming back now," I said. "That motor-cycle guy, Paul-and-Silas." Just then, the door opened, and who should stick his head in, but the motorcycle guy.

I hid under the sheet.

20

"Come on in, Paul-and-Silas," Biggie said. "He's awake now."

I peeked out from under the blanket.

Paul-and-Silas came and stood by my bed, grinning down at me. I was mighty scared and must of showed it because Biggie let out a big hee-haw.

"It's okay, J.R.," she said. "Paul-and-Silas is on our team. Matter of fact, if our little Tennessee cousin hadn't been on the job, you and Monica might not be here."

If I didn't know Biggie better, I'd of thought there was a catch in her voice.

"Biggie, what happened?"

"Yeah," Monica said. "We thought he was a bad guy. Heck, in all the movies the biker is always the bad guy."

"Well, honey," Biggie said, "sure as hell's hot, this is no movie."

"Biggie, what happened?"

"The judge and Chief Trotter kidnapped you," Biggie said.

"See, J.R.? I told you it was the judge," Monica said. "I smelled his cigar, Miss Biggie. I told J.R., I said, 'That there was the judge toting me.' Didn't I say that, J.R.?"

"Yeah, you said it," I said. "But the chief? Biggie, are you sure?"

"Yep," Biggie said. "The Texas Rangers and the FBI have him in jail over at Center Point this very minute. Kidnapping is a federal offense. Yessiree, Travis Trotter's in big trouble. Too bad. Travis never was mean—kind of sneaky and a big liar, but not mean—just too dumb to pour pee out of a boot with the instructions printed on the heel."

"What about the judge?" Monica asked. "He was downright rough with me. Like to of broke my leg. I hope they hang him from the neck until dead."

"They got him, too," Rosebud said. "Last I seen of him, he was talking his head off all the while them Rangers was slappin' the cuffs on him, allowing as how he knew the governor, and he'd have their jobs if they didn't turn him loose."

"Biggie, they won't really hang him, will they?" I asked.

"Of course not, J.R.," Biggie answered. "We don't hang people anymore—but sure as shootin' he'll be put away for a good long time."

"Why'd they do it, Biggie?"

"Just like we suspected," she said. "They were after my land. What we didn't know was, there was a fight between the judge at the courthouse and the mayor and Norman Thripp over at city hall over who was going to outsmart Biggie Weatherford first."

"That'll be the day," Rosebud said under his breath.

"You're right about that, Rosebud," Biggie said. "Better folks than them have tried it. You see, honey, it started when the city went out to start excavating for the dump. The bulldozers found the soft-coal deposit under the Plummer place.

Mayor Gribbons thought it might be valuable, so they contacted an expert from a coal company in West Virginia."

"I'll bet it was Mr. Crabtree."

"You win. Crabtree Energy Company of West Virginia. Well, Crabtree came to town to take the leases, but, of course, they told him right off that I'd never lease, so he pretended to be a burial-policy salesman."

"On account of you own so much land?"

"Yep. They had to have my land to make it worthwhile to mine the coal, seeing as how I own most of the land in that part of the county."

"Biggie," Monica said, "how'd the judge get into it?"

"I'm not sure," Biggie said, "but I suspect it was when Crabtree started filing the leases at the courthouse. The judge found out about it. Then greed took over, and he decided to get in on some of that money himself."

"How?"

"By the most direct route—through me."

"You mean like cozying up to you and getting you to marry him?" Monica said.

"Nope. That wouldn't have worked. I wasn't about to let them mine my property, married or single. Pretending to like me was just a cover, I expect. That way he'd be able to keep tabs on my activities."

"That's where I came in," Paul-and-Silas said. "It was a matter of public record that the original J. R. Wooten had a family back in Tennessee. What they did was to put an ad in the Memphis and Nashville papers asking for descendants of J. R. Wooten, originally of Robertson County, Tennessee. I saw the ad and came west to see what was up. They gave me a plausible story about how I might have a claim on Miss Biggie's holdings but kept me in the dark as to their value. I decided to do a bit of investigating on my own."

Willie Mae came in with a tray full of sandwiches.

"How you kids doin'?" she asked. "Want me to get y'all some soup?"

"How about some ice cream," I said. "Ice cream would make me feel a whole bunch better."

"Me, too!" Monica said.

Willie Mae looked at Biggie.

"Sure," said Biggie with a grin. "How about some of Willie Mae's angel food cake to go with it?"

"No'm. I'll probably never eat angel food cake again as long as I live after seeing Mayor Gribbons's face the night he died. By the way, how *did* he die?"

"Well, they almost got me on that one," Biggie said. "Cyanide was what finally did him in. But the fact remained that somebody had switched his heart pills. It would have been a lot neater if he'd just died of a heart attack. What I had to figure out was who wanted him dead and who had the opportunity to switch pills on him."

"Uh-huh."

"Say 'Yes, ma'am.' Pigs grunt; people talk."

"Yes, ma'am."

"I'd found out from old Plumley that ephedrine is used in treating asthma. Does that mean anything to you?"

I was beginning to catch on. "You bet! Jimmie Sue had it. She had an attack and had to go home the night the mayor died."

"That's right. That's what she and the chief said, anyway." Biggie took a sip of coffee. "What really happened was she slipped around back to create a diversion while the judge put the cyanide in Popolus's whipped cream. Remember Mr. Popolus told us the judge had gone into the kitchen looking for an ashtray—and while he was there Popolus had heard a noise out back and went to investigate?"

"Miss Biggie," Monica said, "how you know all this?"

"You might say, that came from *my* detecting," Rosebud said. "Me and J.R. picked up some mighty valuable clues out behind the café the next day."

"Yes," Biggie said. "Remember that little square bit of glass you brought back?"

"That was me!" I said. "That was *my* clue, Rosebud—not yours!"

Rosebud grinned and folded his arms over his chest.

"Remember when Jimmie Sue visited me at the hospital?" Biggie went on.

"Yes'm."

"Remember her asking me for the time—said her watch was in the shop?"

"Uh-huh, I remember."

"Pigs—"

"Yes, ma'am."

"Well, I took that little piece of glass down to the jeweler, told him I'd found it on the table after the planning meeting. Bless Pat if it wasn't Jimmie Sue's watch crystal!"

"So that's who I heard running off when I went back there that night," I said.

"Probably so. Willie Mae, pass me one of those sandwiches, egg salad, I believe."

"So, Miss Biggie," Monica said, "who switched the mayor's pills? Don't seem to me like Jimmie Sue'd have much chance to do that."

"The chief did. He was so eaten up with love for Jimmie Sue he'd of done anything she asked him to."

"So Jimmie Sue and the judge planned the whole thing?"

"Not exactly, honey. Just the men were in on it at first. Jimmie Sue came into it later. When they found the lignite under the dump, Crabtree sent his engineers here and they tested all the land around there. The richest vein of coal was under Wooten land, and they knew I'd never lease or sell. If they were going to get my coal, they'd have to get rid of me—and you."

"Me?"

"You're my only heir, J.R. My will states that, should you die before me, my land goes to the Daughters to build a retirement community. It would have been easy for a crook like the judge to finagle the papers to fix it so they could steal the mining rights before the Daughters ever knew what happened. It would have worked, too, if Jimmie Sue hadn't gotten in the way."

"How'd she do that?"

"By listening in on telephone conversations and reading the judge's mail, I expect. Remember, she acted as the judge's secretary as well as deputy county clerk. My guess is, once she found out what the judge was up to, she invited herself to the party. Then Paul-and-Silas came to town, and she saw her chance to take it all."

"How's that, Miss Biggie?" Monica asked.

"Easy, she *thought*. She'd just marry Paul-and-Silas, then get rid of me—probably more cyanide. Without me watching after you, you'd be a cinch to get rid of."

"But she said—"

"I know. She claimed Paul-and-Silas was stalking her."

"That's a laugh," Paul-and-Silas said. "I couldn't get away from her. Everywhere I'd go, she'd be there, smiling and waving her cute little fanny. I was flattered at first, but suspicious. Why would the prettiest girl in town be interested in a poor vagrant cyclist?"

"Reckon you was a whole lot smarter than what she given you credit for," Rosebud said.

"Guess so. When I rebuffed her advances, she told the chief I was stalking her. I, being a born coward, decided the better part of valor was to lie low for a while."

"And that," Biggie said, "was when Jimmie Sue decided

it was high time I took advantage of that burial policy old Crabtree had sold me. She tried to hurry me on my way with an ephedrine-flavored milk shake. Silly girl!"

"So, Paul-and-Silas," Monica said, "that was you riding your bike out by the pit last night?"

"It was me all right," he said. "I was standing at the hot-dog stand eating my dinner and chatting with Jimmie Sue when she excused herself and went to get more weenies out of the cooler. When the commotion began at the dunking booth, I slipped around back to see what was going on. I saw it all: Jimmie Sue with the bloody skewer and the men carrying you kids off."

"Why didn't you stop them? Could you tell who it was?" Monica asked.

"Oh, yes. I knew them all right, only, shameful as it is to admit, I'm not as tough as I look. Actually, I'm something of a sissy." Paul-and-Silas blushed. "I jumped on my bike and followed the truck, at a safe distance, of course, and watched from behind a tree while they hurled you into the pit."

"Why didn't you get us out?" Monica asked.

"Because I had no way of bringing you both back to town. I heard you talking below, so I knew you couldn't be badly hurt. I decided the best thing to do would be to come back to get help. I ran into Rosebud and Willie Mae purchasing tickets for the Tilt-A-Whirl and told them of your abduction."

"That's right," Biggie said, "and when they came to me, I had already called Sheriff Stacy over in Center Point. He called in the Texas Rangers."

"You'd *already* called the law?" Monica said. "But how did you know . . ."

Biggie took a big bite of sandwich and chewed real slow, making us wait. Then she took a sip of tea. "Oh," she said, "I knew as soon as the séance was over. Remember when

Jimmie Sue started to get up and the judge pulled her back down?"

"Sure," Monica said. "I remember thinking what a sissy she was."

"When I saw the look on both their faces, I *knew*," Biggie said. "The séance had been a success."

"What about Mr. Thripp?" I asked. "Did they arrest him, too?"

"No, honey. Norman Thripp didn't really do anything— not that he wouldn't steal the pennies off a dead man's eyes given half the chance. He'll probably marry Mattie McClure and that's punishment enough to my way of thinking. Of course, I'll see to it he never works for our city government again." She giggled. "Maybe he'll just have to wait tables at the tearoom."

"Miss Biggie," Willie Mae said, "I thought of something. Who done blowed up that there Crabtree's car?"

"That was a hard one," Biggie said. "J.R. had told me the chief was talking to Jimmie Sue on the phone when he arrived at the station. That threw me off at first, because I naturally assumed she was at the courthouse when she was talking to him—at work like she should have been."

"She was, Biggie," I said. "I saw her come out with her lunch and sit down on a bench."

"That's right," Paul-and-Silas said. "She did come out of the courthouse, but she hadn't been there long, because I saw her walking fast from the direction of your house not five minutes before. She must have been talking to the chief from the pay phone in front of the drugstore—"

"To tell him the deed was done!" Biggie said.

"But why, Biggie?"

"To scare him off, of course. Crabtree knew too much, and was apt to ask for more of the profits than our greedy local citizens were willing to give."

"So when he wouldn't scare so easy, I reckon she just got it in her head to kill him," Rosebud said.

Suddenly I thought of something. "Biggie, where's Jimmie Sue?"

"Nobody knows, honey. The Rangers set up a roadblock around town real soon after Crabtree was killed. They checked every car coming and going. Don't you worry your little head about it. If I'm not mistaken, the Rangers will have her in custody before morning." She came over and stood by my bed. "Now why don't you and Monica try and get some rest. Willie Mae's making smothered steak for supper with mashed potatoes and gravy. Lemon pie for dessert."

Biggie was wrong. The Rangers didn't have Jimmie Sue in custody that morning—or the next.

21

ONE YEAR LATER

This year's festival was a big success. Biggie decided the theme should be "The Yellow Rose of Texas." Butch sent off all the way to Taiwan for a whole trainload of yellow plastic roses to decorate the town. He says the ones left over will make great permanent memorials out at the cemetery.

The Clem Clawson Shows came back this year. I promised Monica I'd go with her to see that half man/half woman she didn't get to see because of not having enough money last year. She saved up all year so she could pay for both of us to get in this time around.

On the day before the parade, Biggie made me go with her down to the tearoom so she could have a meeting with Miss Mattie (who is now Mrs. Norman Thripp) and some of the other Daughters.

"Come on, J.R.," she said. "You got your hair combed?"

"Yes'm." I was sitting in the kitchen watching Willie Mae chop onions.

"You ain't neither," Willie Mae said. "Git in that bathroom and comb your head."

When I got out, Biggie was already on the front porch.

"We'll walk," she said. "Step lively, now. We're meeting Lonie and Ruby Muckleroy for lunch."

"I don't see why I have to go," I said.

Biggie answered real slow, like she was talking to a retarded person or something. "Because, J.R., we are discussing something very important. The Daughters down at state headquarters in Austin have decided to erect a plaque on the grounds of the state capitol dedicated to James Royce Wooten." She stopped and took both my hands in hers, looking me square in the eyes. "The local chapter is responsible for designing it—that's what we have to talk about. Someday you'll be glad you were a part of this—so stop that whining and get a move on!"

I knew when I was licked. "Yes'm."

Mrs. Moody was out in front of her house pinching dead blooms off her hydrangeas. "Hey, Biggie," she said. "Y'all going to town?"

"Sure are," Biggie said without slowing down, "and we don't have time to chat this morning. We're already late for a meeting."

"I don't plan to keep you," Mrs. Moody said. "I was just wondering if y'all would mind picking up Prissy's prescription at the drugstore on the way back."

Biggie stopped. "Since when has Dedrick Plumley taken to filling dogs' prescriptions?"

"Oh, it ain't exactly a dog prescription," Mrs. Moody said. "Prissy's not been herself lately, wheezing a lot and just lying around all day. She even let Booger eat out of her food dish this morning." She squatted down and picked up Prissy, who had been asleep under the hydrangea. Prissy growled at her. "Hush now," Mrs. Moody said, and turned to Biggie. "So, anyway, the vet over in Center Point said I should give her ephedrine. Mr. Plumley ordered it special just for Prissy. It's all ready; all you'd have to do is just pick it up for me."

"Sure, Essie," Biggie said. "We'll drop it off on our way back home. I expect Prissy will be good as new before you know it."

When we got to Miss Mattie's tearoom there stood Mr. Norman Thripp behind the cash register wearing a ruffledy apron.

" 'Morning, Norman," Biggie said. "That's very becoming."

Mr. Thripp didn't say anything, just picked up two menus and led us to a big table in back where Miss Lonie and Mrs. Muckleroy were already seated. Miss Mattie was perched on the edge of a chair at one end of the table like a chicken standing on one leg. Biggie pulled out a chair and sat at the head of the table.

"Norman, you take the orders," Miss Mattie said, "and you'll have to handle everything else for a bit. We're having a committee meeting."

"Yes, dear," said Mr. Thripp.

"Don't thith town jutht look a thight?" Miss Lonie said. "I've never theen tho many yellow rotheth."

"Bee-u-ti-ful!" Miss Mattie said.

"Personally, I think it's a little too much," Mrs. Muckleroy said. "I mean, did he have to hang them from the pecan trees around the square? I think that's overdoing it. After all, isn't the pecan the state tree of Texas already?"

"What are you wearing for the parade, Biggie?" Miss Mattie asked.

"Yellow satin," Biggie said. "Now, let's get down to business. Suppose we put 'James Royce Wooten, Father of Northeast Texas' on the plaque?"

"Well," Mrs. Muckleroy said, "I think it should say 'Muckleroy' on there somewhere. After all, he married a Muckleroy, didn't he?"

They talked on and on while I counted the tiles in the ceiling. There are three hundred and sixty-one not counting the split ones. Finally, they all picked up their purses and stood up.

Miss Lonie sighed. "Well," she said, "I thirtainly hope our fethtival ith happier than latht year—two murderth! Oh, my heart ith jutht going to beat the band thinking about it!"

"And that Jimmie Sue getting away like she did," said Miss Mattie. "Do you think they'll ever catch her, Biggie?"

"Oh, they'll catch her," Biggie said. "The Texas Rangers always get their man."

"I thought that was the Mounties, Biggie," I said.

Biggie looked at her watch. "One Texas Ranger is worth ten Canadian Mounties," she said. "Come on, J.R., we've got things to do. Don't you want to drive out to the farm and bring Monica in to spend the night?"

"We don't have to this year," I said. "Her daddy's driving her in on the tractor tomorrow. He said she ain't much, and kind of funny looking, but she's the only girl he's got and he ain't taking any chances on her falling into any more holes."

That night at supper, I told Biggie about Monica saving the money for us both to go to the freak show. I left out the part about the him/her person.

"Biggie, they've got a fortune-teller, and a petrified man this year," I said. "I saw it on the poster. He's all turned to stone except for his head and one little spot on his stomach. They'll even let you touch him!"

"That ain't nothin'," Rosebud said. "I once seen a man turned to brass—all but his eyes. They had to polish him every day with vinegar and salt or else he'd tarnish and turn green. Now *that* was something to see."

"Humph!" Willie Mae said.

"And they've got a tattooed, bearded belly dancer," I said. "Ever see one of those, Rosebud?"

"Nope," Rosebud said, "but I once seen a man had lumps all over him. His hair jest grew out in little sprigs in betweenst them lumps. Elbert Fontenot, his name was. He's dead now."

"Well, we'd better get to bed soon," Biggie said. "Big day tomorrow."

The parade was a big success. Everybody said it was better than last year even though the Mooslah Temple couldn't come on account of their wives wouldn't let them on account of getting in jail two years in a row. The Daughters entered a float all covered in yellow roses. Butch rode on top dressed as the original Yellow Rose of Texas.

"Most people don't know she was a mulatto from Calcasieu Parish," Rosebud said. "Come to Texas to make the soldiers happy."

"Hush, Rosebud," Biggie said.

As soon as we could get away, me and Monica hightailed it to the midway.

"What do you want to do first?" I asked.

"J.R., I've just got to see that person—you know."

"Yeah, I know. But what if, uh, 'it's' not here this year?"

"Let's go see. Come on!" She was pulling me by the sleeve.

We looked all up and down the midway, but there was no sign of it.

"I want to see the petrified man," I said.

Monica's lip was sticking out a mile. "I don't care," she said.

The petrified man was sitting on a big chair made out of logs. The barker said the last time he was weighed, he weighed one thousand pounds. "He'd split a standard chair like a toothpick! He's made of solid stone. Who'd like to come up and touch the petrified man?"

Before I knew what was happening, Monica had said, "I will!" and was scrunching through the crowd.

The barker lifted her up and held her while she touched the man's finger. "Oowee," she said. Just as he was setting her down, she reached out real quick and touched his toe. She opened her mouth to say something, but the barker shoved her back into the crowd before she could speak.

"His hand felt like stone, but his toe just felt like plain old meat," she said. "I think he's a fake."

Now the barker was holding up a jar containing a pickled baby pig and telling everybody about the real babies they had in back.

"Want to see the fortune-teller?" I asked.

"Naw," said Monica. "It's all just lies anyway. Let's go ride the rides."

Just as we were turning to leave, the man announced the bearded, tattooed belly dancer.

"Wait," I said. "I want to see this."

"Oh, okay," Monica said. "But she's probably a fake, too. Probably all her tattoos are just decals."

Now the music was starting and the lights went down real low. It was hard to tell that anyone was on the stage.

"More light!" someone yelled from the back of the tent, and the lights got a little brighter. We moved up to the edge of the stage.

She sure was tattooed all right. She had little flowers all around her belly where her skirt came down below her navel. Vines grew up her legs, and on her chest she had a pair of lovebirds holding a red heart in their beaks. Her hair was blond and her face was covered with curly, blond hairs. She wasn't a very good dancer, but there was something about her that made me want to keep watching.

"Come on, J.R." Monica said. "I want to go on the Ferris wheel."

"In a minute," I said, inching closer to the stage.

Then I saw it. Her feet were bare and jingly bracelets surrounded her ankles. As I leaned in closer, I saw something that made me turn cold all over. Six toes on her left foot, each toenail painted bright red! Then I looked up at her face, and the eyes that looked at me over that beard were unmistakable. I started in shaking like a hen in a dust bath.

"Let's go," I shouted, grabbing Monica by the hand. "We've got to find Biggie—fast!"

It was Jimmie Sue all right. They arrested her that very night. I never saw her again, but Biggie said when they found her, she'd washed off all her tattoos and taken off her false beard. I couldn't help remembering how pretty she'd been and how nice she'd always been to me. But then I thought about how she murdered Mayor Gribbons and, even worse, Ralph, and how she'd looked at me the night she stabbed Mr. Crabtree. Then I was glad Biggie had solved the crime and the Rangers had taken her off to jail.

Tomorrow, me and Rosebud and Willie Mae and Biggie are going to Wooten's Creek and fish all day long. Biggie says there's nothing like a day on the creek to wash the cobwebs out of your head.

Willie Mae's Special-Occasion Gumbo

The day before, boil you up a nice hen or two large fryers. Save them in the broth they're cooked in.

Make you a roux with one cup vegetable oil and one cup flour. Cook it in a heavy pot until the color of a new copper penny. (Willie Mae used to use lard until Rosebud came down with the high blood.)

Add in: 3 yellow onions, chopped
4 cloves chopped garlic
1 small stalk celery, chopped
2 green bell peppers, chopped

Stir 'til wilted.

Add your broth off your chicken (about two quarts), 1 T salt, some worcestershire sauce, some Tabasco sauce (Rosebud likes about a tablespoonful, but be careful. It's hot!)

Next you add in your chicken cut up in pieces and a pound of smoked sausage cut in slices or some ham if you've got it. Let this simmer for about two hours. Add some more broth or water to the pan if it ain't juicy enough.

Add: 1 pound raw shrimp, peeled
1 pint oysters with juice
1 pound crabmeat, if you've got it

Cook for fifteen minutes more.

Take your pot off the stove and add in 3 T filé powder. Put some cooked rice in a bowl and add your gumbo over it. Serve plenty of french bread for dunking.

(Willie Mae says you can make it with just chicken or just shrimp, but it won't be special-occasion gumbo then.)

READ ON FOR AN EXCERPT OF *BIGGIE AND THE MANGLED MORTICIAN*, THE NEXT MYSTERY BY NANCY BELL FEATURING BIGGIE AND THE PRECOCIOUS J.R.....

1

When I woke the next morning, the sun was shining in my face. My cat, Booger, was sitting on the windowsill watching a nest of baby blue jays outside in the crepe myrtle tree. His tail flicked back and forth like the pendulum on Biggie's grandfather clock. I jumped out of bed and pulled on the jeans I'd worn yesterday and my Houston Rockets T-shirt. It was Saturday, and I had big plans for the day.

When I came down to breakfast, I found Willie Mae standing by the stove making buckwheat cakes, which I think taste like grass clippings but I wouldn't dare tell Willie Mae that.

"Where's Biggie?" I asked.

"Good mornin' to you, too," Willie Mae said. "She be in

her room gettin' ready to go back down to that there Hair House to finish up with her shampoo and set. You want one of these hotcakes?"

"Uh-uh," I said.

"Who you sayin' 'uh-uh' to?"

"No, ma'am," I said.

"Want me to fix you a egg?"

"I'm having Fruit Blasters this morning," I said.

I opened the cabinet door and got the cereal down. Willie Mae set a bowl and a spoon on the table.

"You gonna rot out your teeth and stunt your growth," she said.

Just then, the screen door slammed and Rosebud came in.

"Oo-eee! Hotcakes," he said. "Sweet thing, you must of been readin' my mind."

"How many you want?" Willie Mae asked.

"Six for starters—then we'll see after that." He rumpled my hair with his hand. "What you plannin' to do today, young'un?"

"Watch cartoons, work on my space shuttle model, and build a space station in the chinaberry tree out back," I said. "Will you help me with that, Rosebud?"

Rosebud took a big bite of hotcake and washed it down with some of that black Louisiana coffee he likes so well.

"Did I ever tell you about that time I was workin' for them space folks down in Houston?" he asked.

"You worked for NASA? I didn't know that," I said.

"Sure as I was born a Baptist," he said. "Them space guys wouldn't make a move without consultin' me. I was gonna ride up in one of them things, but at the last minute, the feller that runs the mission control room came down with the stomach flu. If I hadn't of taken over his job, they'd of had to abort the mission."

"Gosh!" I said.

"Rosebud," Biggie said from the doorway, "if you'd done all the things you say you've done, you'd be a hundred and thirty years old."

Rosebud just grinned and held out his plate for more hotcakes. "I'll help you this afternoon," he said. "This morning, I believe I'll just amble on down to the bait shop and see if I can win me a few bucks at dominoes."

Willie Mae was wiping the griddle with a paper towel. She glared at Rosebud. "You ain't goin' to no bait shop," she said. "You're going to stay right here and move the furniture so I can wax the floors." She looked at me. "And you ain't gettin' in my way watchin' cartoons and makin' models. I want everybody out of this house while I'm waxin'."

"You can go with me to the beauty shop," Biggie said. "You can play with little DeWayne."

That wasn't a totally bad idea. DeWayne has a video game in the back room of the shop called "Raiders of the Planet of Doom" which I'm trying to beat him at. The only thing DeWayne can do well is video games on account of he plays them all the time because his mama and aunt Vida won't let him out of the shop that much. DeWayne has already got to level three while I'm still trying to get out of the cave of the saber-toothed android.

"Okay," I said.

We could smell Miss Itha's beauty shop before we even got the door open. It smells good, like shampoo and hair spray and stuff. I heard the ladies talking over the roar of the hair dryer. Itha's House of Hair is a long, narrow building like most of the stores along the square. In back, facing the door, are two black shampoo bowls with chairs to match. Everything else in the whole place is pink and lavender, including the floor tiles and the big dryers and work stations along both the long walls. Butch was giving himself a manicure at the little table near the front door.

Miss Itha was busy putting rollers in Mrs. Muckleroy's hair and Miss Lonie Fulkerson was waiting her turn. Miss Vida was in back shampooing somebody, but I couldn't tell who it was. All I could see was Miss Vida's big behind. She was bending over and you could see the backs of her big white knees spilling over the tops of her hose like Willie Mae's bread dough, and her little-bitty feet that looked like they'd break holding up all that weight.

"Come on in, you all," Miss Itha said. "I'll get to you quick as I can, Biggie. I'm busier than a pair of jumper cables at a tent revival. Vernice was supposed to help me, but she came down with a hangover this morning due to being at the dance at the V.F.W. hall until all hours last night."

"Who's that under the dryer?" Biggie wanted to know. She bent down and peered at the person. "Oh, it's Meredith Michelle. What in the world is that all over her head?"

"It's some extra-large rollers," Mrs. Muckleroy said. "As you no doubt know, Meredith Michelle won Miss Job's Crossing last fall and will be going on to the Miss Ark-La-Tex pageant in Texarkana. If she wins there, it's on to Miss Texas in San Antonio!"

"So, what's with the big rollers?" Biggie wanted to know.

"Big hair, honey," Miss Itha said. "You know, you got to have big hair to win in Texas. It's the law or something."

I finally got a word in. "Is DeWayne here?" I asked.

"No, honey. He's at the dentist." Miss Itha said.

"Can I play with his video game?"

"It's broke," Miss Vida said over her shoulder. "He left it out in the middle of the floor, and I stepped on the thing. Busted it clean in two."

"I'm designing her dress," Butch said.

"What?" Biggie said.

"Her dress for the pageant. I'm designing it."

Biggie sat down in the empty dryer chair. "Has she got a talent?" she asked.

Miss Lonie spoke up. "Talent? Honey, that girl'th jutht oothing with talent."

"You could have fooled me," Biggie said. "What's she going to do?"

"Well," Mrs. Muckleroy said, "we can't decide between a dramatic reading or a song. She can do both equally well."

"Oh, a dramatic reading," Miss Lonie said. "Much more cultural. Don't you think tho, Biggie?"

Biggie shrugged. "I didn't know culture had much to do with it," she said.

"I think she should sing," Butch said, waving his hands around to dry the polish. "Do y'all like this color?" He didn't wait for an answer. "I can design a nice dress for a musical number. Don't know about the dramatic reading. It would depend on what it *was*, don'cha know. I'd hate for her to do that dreadful Scarlett O'Hara 'turnip speech.' No fun making a costume for that!"

"It would be taken from William Faulkner's 'As I Lay Dying,' Mrs. Muckleroy said. "She'd be wheeled out on stage in a pine coffin. Then she'd sit up, gracefully step onstage to do her reading. Either that, or she'll sing 'I Enjoy Being a Girl.'"

Miss Vida finished shampooing her customer and wrapped a towel over her head. The customer was Miss Julia Lockhart, who writes a column for the newspaper.

"How do y'all like your new preacher?" she asked Biggie.

"Rector," Biggie said. "In our church, we call them rectors. He's awfully young."

"I agree," said Mrs. Muckleroy. "Too young for his own

good is what I say. A clergyman should have a little age on him."

"Well, I think he'th jutht awfully cute," Miss Lonie said.

"Me, too," Butch said.

"At least he's making himself useful directing the operetta," Biggie said. "He's very experienced, you know."

"How's that?" Miss Itha asked. "You want some hair spray, honey?" she said to Mrs. Muckleroy.

"Lots," Mrs. Muckleroy said. "I want this hairdo to last a while."

"He wrote, directed, and starred in his class play in seminary," Biggie said. " A musical version of *The Exorcist*."

"That'th right," Miss Lonie said. "He played the demon becauthe it had all the good lineth."

"It got written up in *Anglican Digest*," Biggie said.

Miss Julia was sitting up straight in the shampoo chair rummaging around in her purse. Finally, she said, "Itha Ray, hand me one of them combs and I'll be gettin' the tangles out while I wait. Did y'all hear about Larry Jack?"

"What about Larry Jack?" Biggie asked.

"He's sold the funeral home. He's moving to Houston," she said.

"I'm not surprised that boy is going on to bigger and better things," Butch said. "He could lay out a beautiful corpse. Remember the job he did on poor old Mr. Watson?"

"Ooh, yeth," Miss Lonie said. "Tho thad. Mithter Watthon wath a good bricklayer, too. I'll never underthtand why he hired poor Hoppy Bland to work for him. Everybody knowth Hoppy ain't right bright."

"How'd the accident happen?" Miss Vida asked.

"He was raising a load of bricks up to the roof to make a new chimney for the Hank Furgusons," Biggie said. "They had a pulley up in the oak tree, and Hoppy was supposed to have hitched the rope to a limb but he didn't do that.

Instead, he decided to hold on to the rope. It slipped out of his hands and the whole load fell right on Old Man Watson's head."

"Mashed his head right flat," Miss Julia said.

"Anyway," Butch said, "when Larry Jack got through with him, Mr. Watson looked just like Cary Grant. Now that there's pure-dee artistry."

"Why's he leaving?" Itha wanted to know.

"Business, honey," Miss Julia said. "Larry Jack says there's more business in a day in Houston than you can get in a year here. They're always shooting each other and driving over each other with their cars down there."

"Who's going to take over the funeral home?" Mrs. Muckleroy asked.

"It's a big mystery," Miss Julia said. "All Larry Jack will say is, we'll all be surprised when the new undertaker comes to town. Itha, you'd better look after Meredith Michelle. She's getting mighty red under that dryer."

Miss Vida went and pulled the big hood off Meredith Michelle, who looked like a boiled lobster.

"Can I watch DeWayne's tee-vee?" I asked.

"Sure, honey," Miss Itha said. "You just go on back there."

I watched *Super Heros From Mars*, and an old movie, *Flash Gordon and the Mole People* before Biggie stuck her head around the curtain that separates the back from the front. Her face was all pink and she had little-bitty curls all over her head. She sure didn't look like Biggie who mostly just pulls her hair back in a knot with little curls escaping all around her face. I made a face.

"I went and let Itha talk me into getting a cut and a permanent," she said. "Never mind, it'll grow. Come on, Willie Mae's got lunch ready by now."

While Biggie was paying her bill, I happened to look out

the window in time to see a big black car pull into a parking space right in front of the shop and the ugliest man I'd ever seen get out and start toward the beauty shop. He had broad shoulders and long arms and a face that looked like it had been run over by a bulldozer. He came up to the window and shaded his face with both hands and peered into the shop. I guess Miss Itha saw him too because she dropped the pen she was holding and let out a little holler.

"What's wrong, honey?" Biggie asked, turning toward the window.

Miss Itha couldn't say anything, just kept gasping for breath and pointing toward the window. She was white as Mrs. Moody's little poodle, Prissy.

"Help me get her into a chair, J.R.," Biggie said.

"Vida! Come here. Something's wrong with Itha."

Before you could say boo to a goose, everyone in the shop was gathered around Itha. Miss Julia told her to put her head between her legs. Mrs. Muckleroy wanted to call the doctor. Miss Lonie said a Dr Pepper was the best thing in the world for a fainting spell. Biggie said the best thing was for us to all leave so she could relax. Finally, Miss Vida just picked her up in her arms and carried her to the back of the shop and laid her down on the little daybed they keep back there.

"Y'all can go on home now," she said over her shoulder. "I know what to do."

2

In the "Job's Jottings from Julia" column the next Saturday it said, "Job's Crossing has a new undertaker, Mr. Monk Carter, who is fresh out of mortician's school in Fayetteville, Arkansas. He has purchased the Lively Rest Funeral Home from Larry Jack Jackson, who recently moved to Houston. This writer predicts a great improvement in the appearances of our local dearly beloveds as he is sure to know all the latest 'tricks of the trade.' It is not known why our town's most gifted (and only) hair stylist fell over in a dead faint at the sight of him. Is there something you're not telling us, Itha?"

Biggie read it aloud at the breakfast table. "So that feller was our new undertaker," she said.

"Why do you reckon she did that, Biggie?" I asked. "Miss Itha, I mean."

"Who knows?" Biggie said. She was frowning at the newspaper.

Willie Mae set a big platter of something on the table, then scooped a spoonful on my plate. It looked like scrambled eggs—but not quite.

"Eee-yew," I said, "what's that?"

"That there's Hangtown Fry," she said. "Go on, try it."

I poked it with my fork. "I believe I'll just have cereal."

Rosebud picked up the platter and passed it to Biggie, who helped herself to a big serving of the stuff.

"You havin' some, honey?" he asked Willie Mae.

"You know I don't have nothing to do with oysters," Willie Mae said. "You just go right on and finish it up."

Rosebud emptied the platter onto his plate and took a big bite. "Mm-mm," he said. "I believe I'll have another hot biscuit to finish off with—and some fig preserves."

Biggie passed the preserves, still frowning at Miss Julia's column. "That Julia has been reading Liz Smith again," she said. "Somebody ought to tell her she's no New York gossip columnist. She's going to cause somebody some real misery one of these days." Biggie wadded up the paper and threw it in the trash. She looked out the kitchen window. "It's a beautiful day," she said. "I'll bet the perch out at Wooten's Creek are hungry enough to eat the tail off a dead skunk. I'd give two Sundays in a row to be out there pulling them in."

"Let's go, Biggie," I said.

"Can't, son. Did you forget? I'm giving a garden party tomorrow to kick off the museum's fund drive."

Willie Mae poured fresh coffee in Biggie's cup and handed it to her. "Turn your burners down," she said. "This house is done cleaned up—and Rosebud got the yard lookin' like a golf course."

"Well—" Biggie said.

Before she could finish, me and Rosebud were heading out to the garage to get the fishing poles and tackle ready. We loaded them in the car while Biggie and Willie Mae washed up the dishes. Biggie came out of the house wearing a big red straw hat. She looked like a thumb tack on account of she's not much over four feet tall.

"You drive, Rosebud," she said, "and Willie Mae and I will sit in the back. J.R., you ride up front and hold the poles out the window."

On the way to Wooten's Creek, we passed Biggie's farm where my friend, Monica Sontag, lives with her parents. They rent the farm from Biggie for a dollar a year plus all the fresh vegetables we can eat.

"Biggie," I said, "can we stop and ask Monica to go fishing with us?"

"They're not home," Biggie said. "They went over to Commerce to take care of some business."

"What kind of business?"

"Monkey business," Biggie said. "Ernestene Sontag's sister, Doreen, is all upset because that sorry husband of hers lost their farm in a cockfight, but that's not the worst part."

"That's real sad all right," Rosebud said. "Puts me in mind of the time Willie Mae's brother lost their daddy's cafe to Snake Eyes Garcia in a—"

"What was the worst part, Miss Biggie?" Willie Mae asked real quick.

Biggie dug down into her everyday fishing purse and pulled out a comb. "Comb your hair, J.R. You look like Prissy Moody." She turned to face Willie Mae. "The worst part," she said, "was the fact that Doreen's husband was booking bets on those poor old roosters. The sheriff of Hunt County tossed him in jail and threw away the key. Poor

Doreen pitched a walleyed fit right out in front of the jail, and before they could get her calmed down, she'd broken out with the shingles all up and down her right side."

"I once cured a man of the shingles," Rosebud said. "Doc Thibadeaux over in Natchitoches said it was the worst case he'd ever seen and he just gave up on the poor feller."

"What'd you do, Rosebud?" I asked.

"It wasn't nothing," Rosebud said. "I just went and taken him down to the banks of the Sabine River and rubbed that old black river mud all over him. After that, I made him set in the sun until the clay dried up harder'n a preacher's, uh—heart." Rosebud slapped his knee and laughed without making a sound. "Lord, if he didn't look a sight with skeeters buzzin' all around him and a witch doctor settin' right smack on his nose."

"Why didn't he just brush it off?"

"Well, sir, he couldn't of done that on account I'd done told him he couldn't move a hair until that clay dried. I'd told him if one single crack come on his body, we'd have to start right back over at the git-go."

"How come?"

"Trade secret, boy. If I told you, you'd go and tell all your friends and then ever'body in Texas would know how to doctor the shingles." He winked at Willie Mae, who was glaring at him from the back seat. "Anyway, after the clay dried, I snuck up behind him and shoved him off the bank into the river. When he come up, all them shingles was gone off his body, and he never had no trouble again. Feller was so grateful, he gimme the best huntin' dog I ever had."

"Whatever happened—"

"Never mind," Biggie said. "Turn here, Rosebud. I want to drive by the Wooten family cemetery and make sure nobody's pushed over any tombstones. I declare, I wish I knew who's been doing that."

"Monica says it's the Wooten Creek Monster," I said. "She said she'd seen his tracks all over the place."

Biggie didn't answer.

"Biggie! Didn't you hear what I said?"

"I heard you," Biggie said. "That kind of talk doesn't require an answer, J.R. You know there's no Wooten Creek Monster."

"But Monica—"

"Drive on, Rosebud," Biggie said. "Everything looks— wait a minute. Stop."

Before Rosebud could get the car stopped all the way, Biggie had jumped out and was trotting down the little gravel path that divided the cemetery. The rest of us followed. Biggie stopped in front of her parents' grave and picked up a green vase that had a bunch of dead flowers in it.

"J.R., go over to that hydrant and fill this with water," she said. "I'm going to pick some of those climbing roses and put them on Mama and Papa's grave. I declare, I didn't know they'd still be blooming here in the middle of October."

I started for the hydrant Biggie had installed for watering the grass but I never made it to fetch that water. What I saw right in the middle of Great Uncle General William B. Travis Wooten's grave made my blood turn to buttermilk. There, in the soft ground, was the biggest footprint I'd ever seen in my whole life. Then I saw another...and another, leading straight into the woods behind the graveyard. Those footprints must of been bigger than a tennis racket and a good six feet apart.

As soon as I could get my feet to move, I ran faster than a duck in a hailstorm back to the others. My mouth hadn't quite caught up with my feet, so I just stood there panting and pointing back where I'd come from.

"Well, I'll be switched," Biggie said when she saw the prints.

"Dog my cats!" Rosebud said.

Willie Mae crossed herself, then began mumbling spells as she gathered pine cones and arranged them in the shape of a triangle in the middle of the biggest print. Next, she found a smooth gray stone and spit on it before placing it in the center of the triangle.

"We'd best be goin'," she said.

For once, Biggie didn't have a thing to say as we all walked back to the car and climbed in.

The sun was high in the sky when we finally drove down to our favorite fishing spot on the creek.

"How 'bout if we eat now?" Rosebud said. "Them fish ain't gonna be bitin' in this heat."

Biggie thought that was a fine idea, so Rosebud got the hamper out of the trunk and I brought along the ice chest which held a gallon pickle jar full of sweetened iced tea with mint leaves floating around in it. Willie Mae spread a tablecloth on the ground under a post oak tree and started to unpack the hamper. We had meat loaf sandwiches made from last night's leftovers and potato salad, bread-and-butter pickles and deviled eggs.

After we finished, Willie Mae walked into the woods to search for roots and herbs to use in her voodoo spells while Rosebud rolled over and fell asleep.

"Biggie," I said, "was Uncle General William B. Travis a real general?"

"No, son. That was his name, General William B. Travis Wooten. The real William B. Travis was a hero in the Texas Battle for Independence. Uncle met a real general once though. That Yankee general—Sherman."

"How?"

Biggie sat up straight. The only thing she likes better than fishing is talking about her ancestors. "Well, Uncle General William B. Travis ran a stagecoach inn up in the Oklahoma Territory. Once the general—he was old then—came through traveling west on the stage. Uncle said he wasn't impressed. By that time Sherman was old and stooped over and had white hair. Uncle General William B. Travis knew Quanah Parker, too. He used to come by the inn every month or so to buy chewing tobacco."

"Who's that?"

"Quanah Parker? He was a great chief—half white. My goodness, J.R., don't they teach you anything in that school?"

"No'm." I decided to change the subject before Biggie decided to educate me herself. "Biggie, where's DeWayne's daddy?"

"What? Oh, well, DeWayne doesn't need a daddy. He's got Vida."

"Biggie—"

Biggie sighed. "J.R., as far as you or anybody else needs to know, DeWayne doesn't have a daddy. My stars! Who taught him to play ball and swim? Who dresses up like Santa Claus every single Christmas—"

"And doesn't even have to wear a pillow," I giggled.

"And who dressed up like a circus clown at his birthday party last year?" she continued.

"I know, Miss Vida."

Biggie smiled. "Right. And who takes him with her every Saturday night when she plays poker out at the Dew Drop Inn? Vida Mae. That's who."

"Biggie, isn't that where he fell out of a tree and broke his collarbone? I don't reckon that's being too good of a daddy. Lettin' him get hurt and all."

"And who walked two miles back to town, carrying him

195

in her own arms, Mr. Smarty?" Biggie stood up and put her red hat back on. "Let's walk down to the creek and drown some worms."

I grabbed our poles and followed Biggie down the slope to the creek. Guess what. Somebody had our fishing spot. A funny-looking woman with two kids was sitting on my very favorite rock fishing. Just as they came in view, the woman pulled her line out of the water with a big old perch just flopping yellow in the sun.

"Well, well," Biggie said. "If it isn't Bettie Jo Darling and her children, Franklin Joe and Angie Jo."

As soon as those two kids heard Biggie's voice, they jumped up and scuttled off into the woods like two possums, their heads poking out in front of them, and their little pale eyes darting from side to side. Their mama looked at the ground, but I thought I saw a smile on her freckled face. The dress she was wearing looked exactly like one Biggie'd worn on Easter Sunday the first year I'd come to live with her in Job's Crossing.

"Biggie, that looks just like—" I pointed to the dress.

Biggie didn't answer, just walked over to the woman and got right up in her face. "Catching anything?" she said, real loud.

When the woman answered, I just about jumped out of my skin. Her voice sounded like somebody practicing the tuba when they didn't know how to play very well.

"Doobicle," she said, and held up a stringer full of fish.

"How—are—the—children?" Biggie asked, still looking right in her face and moving her lips real slow.

"Ustgow ime," the woman boomed.

At that moment, Rosebud came bounding down the hill, looking like he'd just seen the devil. Biggie gave him a look and he stopped twenty feet away and waited. When the woman saw Rosebud, she ran off in the direction her children had gone.

"Biggie, who was that?" I asked.

"Just someone I know," Biggie said. "Don't be nosey. Let's fish."

"She left her fish. Do you reckon she'll come back for them?"

"She'll come back when we're gone," Biggie said. "Rosebud, bring that minnow bucket out of the car. I feel like catching me a big old bass today."

We fished until sundown and came home with a good catch, which Willie Mae fried for supper. After supper, Biggie said she was going to bed early so she could get ready for her party. I went in and sat on the edge of her bed.

"Biggie, can I ask you just one question?"

"Anything, J.R. You know that."

"Why did that woman at the creek sound the way she did?"

"She's deaf, J.R. She hasn't heard the sound of a human voice since she was three years old and lightning took away her hearing—but none of her wits."

"Well, why did her kids run off like that?"

"You said *one* question, and I answered that. Now, get out of here and let me get my beauty rest."

Biggie and the Mangled Mortician—
Now available in hardcover from
St. Martin's Press!

Build yourself a library of paperback mysteries to die for—DEAD LETTER